The Sixth Armada Monster Book

D1323514

THE SIXTH ARMADA

Monster Book

Edited by R. Chetwynd-Hayes

Illustrated by Eric Kincaid

Armada

The Sixth Armada Monster Book was first
published in the U.K. in Armada in 1981 by
Fontana Paperbacks,
14 St. James's Place, London SW1A 1PS.

The arrangement of this collection is copyright
© R. Chetwynd-Hayes 1981.

Printed in Great Britain by
Love & Malcomson Ltd.,
Brighton Road, Redhill, Surrey.

CONTENTS

ACKNOWLEDGEMENTS

The Editor gratefully acknowledges permission to reprint copyright material to the following:

Angus Campbell for *The Mudadora*.
© Angus Campbell 1981.

Henry Glynn for *The Slippity-Slop*. © Henry Glynn 1981.

Keith Timson for *Legend of the Spiders*.
© Keith Timson 1981.

Terry Tapp for *The Bean Rock Monster*.
© Terry Tapp 1981.

Patricia Moynehan for *Monster in Distress*.
© Patricia Moynehan 1981.

Daphne Froome for *Captain Castleton's Biscuit Beetle*.
© Daphne Froome 1981.

R. Chetwynd-Hayes for *The Gale-Wuggle*.
© R. Chetwynd-Hayes 1981.

EDITOR'S NOTE

Every effort has been made to trace the owners of the copyright material in this book. It is the editor's belief that the necessary permission from publishers, authors and authorised agents has been obtained, but in case of any question arising as to the use of any material, the editor while expressing regret for any errors, will be pleased to make the necessary corrections in future editions of the book.

INTRODUCTION

My interest in monsters began on the day I first saw the film *King-Kong*, having convinced the lady in the ticket office that I was over sixteen years of age. I still regard the stand-up fight between Kong and a dinosaur as one of the most exciting action scenes ever filmed. But, alas, we have all grown too sophisticated in recent years and have had a surfeit of giant apes, and dinosaurs, pterodactyls, golems, things from outer space, and nameless horrible wriggly things.

For that reason I have again tried to gather together a collection of quite remarkably horrible monsters in this book.

The first which I recommend for your consideration is *The Mudadora* by Angus Campbell. This creature is a very nasty specimen and not one I would like to meet in a dark wood. Imagine a skeleton that over a long period gradually becomes coated with mud, then acquires a hideous kind of life. How Mr Campbell came to learn about this particular monster, I have not the slightest idea, but I am extremely grateful to him for this graphic, if hair-raising story. I am certain that every monster-lover will find it shudderingly good.

The Slippity-Slop, by Henry Glynn, contains a dire warning. Do not dig deep holes in the garden – there's no way of knowing what you may find, until it is too late. Should you stumble across a large egg with roots, throw it over the fence into the next-door garden and let someone else do whatever is necessary. But under no circumstances put it in the loft – that's the way to finish up with something that slips and slops . . . slips and slops . . .

The Legend of the Spiders, by Keith Timson, is by way of being a science-fiction story and recounts what takes place on a planet far distant in space and time. The spiders of the title are really monsters; gigantic horrors that the hero has the mad idea of riding. That's right. Turning them into multiple-legged horses with mandibles. I am prepared to maintain that some such creature does exist somewhere out there on one of the billion worlds that make up our galaxy.

As everyone is aware, back in the dawn of history any self-respecting prince would consider it his bounden duty to take on a fire-breathing dragon. In *The Prince and the Dragon*, by Andrew Lang, our royal hero proves to be no exception, but how he tackles his monstrous opponent I must leave you find out. Although dinosaurs are supposed to have been long extinct when man first crawled out of the primeval swamp, I am prepared to state that the legend of the dragon has its origin in one of these giant reptiles.

I have always wanted to know why a jumping bean jumps, and am very grateful to Terry Tapp for this priceless piece of information. In *The Bean Rock Monster* we are presented with a really blood-chilling situation that is set against a very convincing Mexican background. One can feel the hot sunshine, see the harsh landscape, and taste the fear which besets the villagers when the Bean Rock monster goes on the rampage.

Monster in Distress, by Patricia Moynehan, has everything needed to excite our interest and maintain it from the first word to the last; a ruined castle, a wicked magician, a detached hand that walks on its fingertips – and, of course, a distressed monster. Our young heroine handles the bizarre situation with undaunted courage and considerable ingenuity, without, of course, any assistance from thick-headed adults, who would not recognise a monster if it sat on the foot of their beds and made faces at them. It all adds up to a very chilling story which should not be read at night in an empty house.

In the days of Nelson's navy, sailors often had to exist for months on a diet of pickled beef and a type of biscuit called "hard tack". After a while the latter was not made any more appetising by a species of maggot known as a weevil. Daphne Froome introduces us to a particularly lethal specimen in *Captain Castleton's Biscuit Beetle*, which is large enough to consume those who were hoping to eat the biscuits. How this creature came into being, and the means by which two children (their father had supplied the biscuits) dispose of it, makes enthralling reading. A very original monster.

And finally there is my contribution. What can I say? Well – firstly it is completely true. Honestly. Go out on a very windy day and look up at the sky. Sooner or later the clouds will assume the shape of a creature with large pointed ears, a grotesque head and two blazing eyes. That will be *The Gale-Wuggle*. And what is more, if you look very carefully, you may discover that what at first appeared to be rooks, are, in fact, little old ladies wearing top-hats and black cloaks. Never take anything for granted. My hero is a sick boy who attracts the attention of the Gale-Wuggle – and other strange beings as well.

So – eight fiendish new monsters. Who could ask for more? I wish you monstrous good reading.

R. Chetwynd-Hayes.

THE MUDADORA

By Angus Campbell

FAR away, in the midst of a dense forest, a skeleton lay half buried under a pile of decaying leaves. How it came to be there, no one will ever know, but it is reasonable to suppose that some poor weary traveller, hopelessly lost in that vast labyrinth of trees, sank down and died through hunger and exhaustion.

Every year the north wind came howling through naked branches, chasing the dead leaves, sometimes uncovering the grinning skull, at others burying it deeper, until finally, after the lapse of many centuries, all that remained was a long mound of bracken-covered compost.

Rain turned earth into mud; sunlight seeped through the forest roof and gave life to primroses and bluebells, which lived out their brief existence in the warm, humid air—then died.

But the sun gradually gave life to something else that did not die.

Deep down under the compost, mud filled the rib cage and skull, formed a thick coating over legs and arms, gained substance from tiny fibrous roots that wormed their way in through fossilised bones and—aided by the sun's warmth—slowly, but so very surely, became a reservoir of seething, primitive life.

One day a long crack went shuddering across the mound; it widened, deepened, became a shallow trench from which a colony of ants poured like terrified citizens from a doomed city. Then it erupted, became a gaping hole, and a monstrous head that glittered with a strange, green, luminous light, came up from the dank, steaming earth. For a while—like a sleeper newly awake—it remained motionless. Then there was a grotesque heaving and a mighty rending sound, as though a million tiny roots were being torn from a long-filled grave. Suddenly IT stood upright—a squat, terrifying figure that rightfully belonged to a half-forgotten nightmare.

There was a rough semblance of legs and arms, but the hands and feet were no more than irregular blobs of congealed mud. Ragged root ends gave the impression that the creature was covered with coarse hair, while the head appeared to be crowned by a damp, matted wig.

Presently it took one faltering step forward—then another—and gradually advanced across the forest floor.

Over the years, this earth-born creature was sometimes seen by charcoal burners, or men whose business took them into wild and lonely places, and they, to a man, ran faster than ever before in their lives. They spoke with hushed voices of what they had seen, and many an embellished story was told round a cottage fireplace, or in the smoke-dimmed bar of a country inn. Gradually this thing of bone, mud and broken roots acquired a name. It was THE MUDADORA ...

"Rosevine" was not a beautiful cottage, or even a picturesque one, being merely a square building with two windows up and two down and a green door in the centre. A once white picket fence was broken by a lopsided gate, which opened on to a cracked cement path that was flanked on either side by an expanse of weed-filled garden. Beyond, like a green and black curtain, was the southernmost fringe of the forest; a great army of trees that curved round into a vast arc, as though preparing to encircle the cottage and eventually bury it under a mass of towering trunks and interwoven branches.

"Well, what do you think of our little retreat?" Mr Carstairs enquired. "Nice and secluded, eh?"

Raymond Carstairs looked first at the looming wall of trees, then wistfully back along the dusty road that led to the distant village.

"Yes, Grandfather," he said. "It's certainly secluded."

"Just the place for a boy to spend a long summer holiday," his grandmother declared. "I can't think how you can stand living in a town with all that noise and smoke."

"No smoke here," Mr Carstairs said, picking up Raymond's case and leading the way into the cottage. "And not much noise either. Only good country sounds, like bird song and the wind whistling through the trees."

Once in the house, Raymond examined the heavy oak sideboard, the well-worn padded chairs and whitewashed walls, with critical interest. He decided the cottage was not only secluded, but primitive as well, and thought wistfully of his parents' comfortable house back in Wolverhampton. Mr Carstairs waited until his wife had retired to the kitchen, then motioned the boy to a chair.

"Now, I understand from your father that you've an important examination to pass next term and he thinks that this is an ideal place for concentration. No distractions and so forth. So I hope you'll work hard, but find time for long walks which will benefit your body and mind."

Raymond thought his grandfather was a bit of a windbag, but nevertheless meant well. So he said politely: "It is very kind of you and Grandma to have me. I will try not to be a nuisance."

Mr Carstairs shook his head in protest.

"You'll never be a nuisance. Quite the contrary. But there is one thing I'd better mention. Don't go wandering off into the forest after sunset. Apart from getting lost, there's always the chance of some wild animal on the prowl after dark."

Raymond experienced the first flicker of interest

11

since he had arrived at Rosevine Cottage. "Wild animal! Here in England?"

The old man shrugged. "I'm not saying there is, but I've heard strange sounds coming from the forest some nights. A sort of coughing bark and once a terrible scream. Don't forget it's less than a hundred years since the last wolf was killed in these parts."

Raymond shot an excited glance out of the window and saw the giant trees nodding their green heads.

"Gosh, a wolf! Do you suppose there are still some left?"

Mr Carstairs rose from his chair. "Most unlikely, but there's certainly something out there, although exactly what, I would not care to say. Now, I expect your grandmother has dinner ready. A nice hotpot."

Raymond undressed by moonlight. This was made possible by the uncurtained window and a full moon, which flooded the room with silver light and would have enabled him to read a book had he been so inclined. It also turned the unkempt back garden and adjacent forest trees into a glorious wonderland where shimmering leaves and shadow-shrouded trunks seemed to rear up from a delicate green sea.

Raymond climbed into bed, pulled the bedclothes up to his chin and pondered on the possibility of getting some sleep. Apart from the brightly-lit room, a series of disturbing sounds did little to enhance the prospect of a restful night. An owl insisted on sending out a mournful hooting noise at irregular intervals; then there was an occasional, peculiar, whirring cry that may have proclaimed the hunting activities of a nightjar, plus the eerie howl of a wild cat.

Once, Raymond sat up in bed as a black fluttering shadow passed over the right-hand wall, and it was some time before he realised it had been caused by a bat flying past his window. He muttered: "If this is the peaceful countryside, give me Wolverhampton," and buried his head under the bedclothes.

He eventually fell asleep; sank down into a dimly-lit dream valley, where black shapeless figures perched on mountain slopes and howled, hooted and screamed a frightful chorus. Then there was one scream that was much louder than the others, an awful shriek of mortal terror. Raymond struggled up from his cocoon of sheets and blankets, sat upright, and stared with dilated eyes at the gleaming window.

The scream rang out again. High-pitched, drawn-out—it came from somewhere just below the window; probably in the garden or on the edge of the forest. Although Raymond was not at all keen to see what was making such a dreadful sound, curiosity made him climb out of bed and walk very slowly towards the window.

The moon had moved a little to the east, but it still highlighted the garden and the encroaching forest. At first, Raymond saw nothing unusual; the summer grass trembling beneath the wind's gentle caress, the softly murmuring trees, the tumultous shadows—the swift passing of a night bird. Then a small shape scurried out from the forest and came to an abrupt halt just below his window.

It was a hare. The long ears stood erect, the grey and white body was so still it might have been carved from stone, and the eyes glittered in the moonlight like fire-flecked rubies. For a while it seemed as if the night was holding its breath. Then, from the dense shadow cast by a giant oak tree, came the sound of—and this was the only description that Raymond could bring to mind—a bubbling cough. He flattened his nose against the windowpane and, by straining his eyes, could just make out a black shape that was barely discernible against

13

the massive tree trunk. The hare turned very slowly and began to crawl back across the garden, moving in a straight line towards that hulking dark mass. It screamed twice more, and Raymond, who could not bear to see animals suffer, pulled up the lower sash of his window and shouted: "Run... run... run!"

The sound of his voice must have broken the spell, for the hare stopped, jerked its head round, then streaked obliquely over the garden and disappeared into the forest. But Raymond felt a thrill of apprehension run down his spine when he became aware of unseen eyes watching him from the dense shadow under the oak tree; the black bulk had not moved, but it did seem as if a head was raised as though it were examining a rash intruder who had cheated a hungry hunter of its chosen prey.

The bedroom door opened and Mr Carstairs entered the room. He was wearing a thick dressing-gown and tasselled nightcap and looked suddenly very old and frightened.

"What's the matter, my boy?" he asked. "I heard you call out."

Raymond spoke over one shoulder. "There's something under a tree. I can't see it very clearly."

His grandfather shuffled with marked reluctance towards the window, then narrowed his eyes and peered down into the moonlit garden.

"I can't see anything. Are you sure you actually saw something?"

"Absolutely positive," Raymond replied with a certain amount of impatience. "Look—over there—under that tree . . ."

He stopped and narrowed *his* eyes, for at that moment a small cloud passed over the moon and it became exceedingly difficult to see if, in fact, there was anything unusual under the trees. Mr Carstairs drew

14

him gently from the window, then led him towards the bed.

"Sit down, my boy, and listen to me. In a lonely place like this it is so easy to be misled by imagination. Maybe I should not have mentioned that I heard strange sounds coming from the forest . . ."

"A bubbling cough," Raymond interrupted. "I heard it myself."

"No doubt you did. And I am certain there is a natural explanation for it. Possibly some wild animal, or maybe a poor mad creature that lives out a precarious existence in the forest. But you must not worry about what you hear, or imagine you see. Just go to sleep and dream of beings that walk upright under the noonday sun."

"But the moonlight," Raymond protested. "It's so difficult to sleep."

Mr Carstairs stared at the naked window, then shook his head in self-reproach. "Of course, how careless of me! I will drape a blanket over the pelmet board, and tomorrow I'll get your grandmother to dig out some nice thick curtains."

The old man took a folded blanket from a drawer in the dressing-table and, assisted by Raymond, hung it over the window. Then he lit a candle, and suddenly the room was an amber-tinted refuge; a haven where sleep was a soft-footed friend, and one need not think about a black motionless something that stood under an oak tree and made a hare scream with terror.

Mr Carstairs smiled down at his grandson.

"Good night," he said softly. "Sleep well."

Raymond was awakened by bird song.

He jumped out of bed, pulled the blanket from the window and looked out upon a world that was bathed in sunlight. Gone were the nasty shadows, the eerie,

15

shuddering movement that is peculiar to even the most beautiful moonlit scene. Neither was there the slightest suggestion of a black shape under the oak tree.

Now the forest appeared to be celebrating the birth of a new day. Branches trembled as though with gentle merriment, leaves applauded the antics of a passing breeze, dandelions nodded their golden heads, and two white butterflies chased each other with thoughtless abandon round a clump of harebells.

Raymond washed and dressed, then ran downstairs, there to be welcomed by the smell of frying eggs and bacon, and the sight of his grandmother's beaming face as she spread a snow-white cloth over the table.

"Did you sleep well?" she asked.

"Yes . . . yes, very well, thank you."

"I was sure you would. Nothing like the peace and quiet of the countryside to make you sleep. Now, sit you down, while I call your grandfather. He's messing about in that shed of his."

But on this particular morning, Mr Carstairs required no prompting, for he came in through the open kitchen doorway and, after sniffing in a most appreciative manner, exlaimed: "That smells good, Martha! I'm that hungry, I could eat a bull—horns and all."

The day started well.

Once breakfast was over and Raymond had helped to wash up and put all the crockery away in the oak dresser, Mr Carstairs looked out of the window and said: "Now I know you must get down to your studies, lad, but what do you say to a nice walk first? Aye? Just to set you up for the day?"

Raymond agreed that this would be very nice, so they both set out, equipped with stout walking sticks and a parcel of ham sandwiches, for Mrs Carstairs maintained they were bound to get hungry and lunch was hours away. Pine needles crunched under their feet;

16

interlocked branches overhead created the impression that the forest was one vast cathedral, where the wind did duty as an organ, and a congregation of birds sang a never-ending song of praise. Sometimes a squirrel sped across the forest floor, then raced halfway up a tree trunk, where it paused and watched the passers-by with bright, inquisitive eyes.

"I like to think," Mr Carstairs said, "that the forest is a great storehouse of primitive life. Birds, animals, insects, every kind of plant imaginable—heavens above knows what is taking place in those trees or under this carpet of dead leaves."

Raymond had not forgotten what *had* taken place the night before.

"You don't suppose we'll meet—whatever it was that made that awful noise last night?"

Mr Carstairs struck at a pine-cone with his walking-stick.

"No—otherwise I would never have brought you out here this morning. The forest during the dark hours is a different place to the one we see now. It is then that the night citizens come out. The fox, screech-owl, nightjar and other creatures that do not love the sunlight. There's a man I would like you to meet. He's a strange body and lives all alone in a small cottage that has been the property of his family for generations."

Some half an hour later found them entering a long, wide dell, where a tiny, stone-walled cottage stood in the centre of a circular clearing. It was only one storey high, with a solitary window and a stout oak door, and appeared—so Raymond thought—to be the kind of place that might well house a warlock or witch. Then he saw round stacks of wood which gave out perpetual plumes of smoke, and assumed that the occupant of this woodland cottage was a charcoal-burner.

Suddenly the door opened and a little, bowed-shouldered man ambled out on to the doorstep and welcomed Mr Carstairs with a gap-toothed grin.

"Good morning to yer, Squire. See's you've brought a young 'un with yer."

"Morning Jasper. This is my grandson, Raymond," Mr Carstairs said. "He's down here for the summer holidays. Thought he might like to see how a real woodsman lives."

The little man pulled his leather jerkin tighter about his muscular body, then stepped to one side.

"Well, if you'd care to step inside, I'll make a cup of summat 'ot. The sun 'asn't 'ad time to warm the glades as yet, and there be a nip in the air."

Raymond discovered that the cottage only had one room, but this was a delightful place which had not been spoilt by broom, brush or duster. The stone floor was covered with dead leaves, a pile of old rags lay in one corner, and bunches of dried herbs hung from the rafters. A table, a narrow bed and a plain wooden chair were the only furniture worth mentioning, but a magnificent collection of stuffed birds, squirrels, badgers and one evil-looking snake, more than compensated for this lack of comfort.

Jasper brushed dust from the chair with the sleeve of his jerkin, waited politely for Mr Carstairs to seat himself, then motioned Raymond to the bed.

"Sit you down there, young 'un. That's right. Now I'll brew some 'erb tea. Put 'airs on yer chest, it will."

He placed a soot-coated pot on the antiquated stove, then gave three earthenware mugs a perfunctory rub with a filthy piece of rag.

"You keeping well, Jasper?" Mr Carstairs asked.

The little man tipped some greenish substance from a tin into a teapot. "Mustn't grumble. Few twinges when the north wind comes a-blowing along the glades."

18

Raymond cleared his throat. "Do you really live here all by yourself?"

Jasper chuckled. "Can't think of a better person to live with, young 'un. Meself don't open the door after sunset, or forget to put up the winter shutter. All being said and done, meself is a pretty reliable chap."

He poured boiling water into the teapot, then nodded with evident satisfaction while Raymond asked a very important question.

"Why . . .why wouldn't you want the door opened after sunset?"

Jasper chuckled again, then poured dark green liquid from the teapot into the three mugs. "Why wouldn't I want the door opened after sunset? he says! Listen to me young 'un. There's things that walk the forest glades at night that would make yer 'air stand on end. Many's a time I've seen chaps in lincoln green a-prancing about in moonlight, and it ain't bothered me none when I could look right through 'em. Then there's the Gale-Wuggle that sort of sinks down through the trees and crouches out there, a-glaring at me winder and daring me to go out. But I be too fly for that. Aye."

Raymond said: "Gosh!" and sipped the hot, mint-flavoured liquid from his mug. Jasper sank down beside him and poked a dirty forefinger into his stomach.

"But there be some things it bain't be good to look upon. Tell me, young 'un. You ever 'eard tell of the-Mudadora?"

Raymond shook his head. "No. Never."

"Aye, it not be much of a ed-u-ca-tion they be giving at them fancy schools. A mighty greet thing, it be. Made from long-dead bones and mud and roots, with green, a-terribly gleaming eyes, and it be powerful hungry. Aye, that it be."

Mr Carstairs rose hurriedly from his chair. "I think we had better be pressing on, Jasper . . ."

19

The little man turned abruptly in his direction. "Like all the rest, yer are. Not wanting to know what gives a bubbling cry in the night. If it 'adn't be for me putting a bit of summat out for it to eat—a couple of ripe rabbits, an 'aunch of dripping venison—it would 'ave been peering in through yer winder long since."

"Yes—well . . ." Mr Carstairs put his mug down on to the table. "I'm sure we're grateful to you, Jasper. But we really mustn't take up any more of your valuable time. Come along, Raymond."

Raymond was not at all sorry to vacate his seat on the bed, and adroitly avoided Jasper's clutching hand that endeavoured to hold him back as they went through the open doorway. The little man shouted after them: "You ought to listen. Game be getting pretty scarce these days, and it be coming out some dark night . . ."

Mr Carstairs grabbed Raymond's arm and pulled him towards the narrow, homeward path.

"Thank you very much, Jasper. We'll call again."

Raymond had not realised that his grandfather could walk so fast, for he all but ran along the path and did not stop until the cottage was hidden by a large clump of trees.

"Really," he said rather breathlessly. "I had not realised the poor fellow was quite like that. Living all alone out here has driven him potty. No other word for it—potty."

"Then you don't think there's such a creature as the—the Mudadora?"

His grandfather tried to laugh, but did not quite make it.

"Of course not. Pure superstition. Mind you, I'm not saying there isn't something very strange that wanders around here at night. But—what was it?—mud and bones? No—it can't be."

But Raymond noticed that the old man said very

little for the rest of their homeward journey and stead-
fastly refused to answer any further questions on the
subject.

The day passed, and night once again stretched out its
arms over forest and countryside. Raymond saw arrow-
shaped formations of birds winging their way across the
sky, as he sat by his bedroom window, vainly trying to
study, and seemed to remember that this was said to be
an omen of a pending storm. Then his grandfather
entered the room carrying a lighted oil lamp, and it was
time to draw the recently hung curtains; once again
create an amber-tinted haven that was far removed
from the sighing forest and the deepening gloom.

"Supper will be ready in no time at all," Mr Carstairs
promised. "How are you progressing with your holiday
task?"

"So and so." Raymond was unwilling to admit he had
hardly done anything at all. "I've sort of got to grips
with it."

"Good boy. By the way, I'm pleased you didn't mention Jasper's nonsense to your grandmother. Lately
she's inclined to be a bit nervous after nightfall. And I
don't want her made worse by talk of this Muddy . . .
Mud . . ."

"Mudadora," Raymond prompted.

"Ah, yes, indeed. So long as we're shut up nice and
snug in here, there's no need to worry about such
things—is there?"

Suddenly Raymond realised that his grandfather was
frightened. Although he was prepared to laugh at
Jasper's warning, dismiss it as the ravings of a near
madman, nevertheless he knew there was something—
perhaps a dreadful something—walking the forest
glades at night. A creature that might even now, be
lurking a few metres beyond the back garden.

21

"Of course, there's nothing to worry us," he said cheerfully. "No wild animal could get in here."

"That's right, my boy. Haven't I always said it was some kind of wild beast that makes those horrible noises?"

But that evening, after supper had been eaten and the dishes washed and stacked away, Raymond watched his grandfather start at the slightest sound and glance anxiously at the window, as though he expected a monstrous head to push its way through the curtains. Then it was time to go to bed, and they all trooped upstairs, each carrying a lighted candle, and Mr Carstairs said—much too heartily: "The moon won't keep you awake tonight. Eh, my boy?"

Raymond agreed it most certainly would not, even while he pondered on a daring—not to mention blood-chilling—idea.

Once in his room, he lay fully dressed on the bed and whispered: "I won't do it. I can't." But curiosity—which is reputed to kill cats—made him change his mind every other minute. Was there really such a creature as the Mudadora? If so, what did it look like?

There was, of course, only one way to find out.

"I'd be mad to go out there all by myself," Raymond told himself over and over again. But suppose he were to creep from the house soon—now, for example—and hide himself behind a bush, then the creature need never know he was there, and curiosity could be satisfied without undue risk.

Without actually realising what he was doing, Raymond slid off the bed and walked on tiptoe towards the door.

Intermittent clouds drifted across the moon and sent their grotesque shadows racing over the garden and into the looming forest. Raymond, now extremely alarmed at his own intrepidity, made himself as comfortable as circumstances permitted behind the foremost bush and decided he would wait for one hour and not a minute longer.

One fact became clear during the first ten minutes. The forest never slept. Apart from the disturbing hoot of an owl, there were distant cries, the perpetual whisper of wind-teased leaves, the patter-patter of tiny feet, and the occasional crack of breaking twigs.

Then a particularly heavy cloud bank laid a thick blanket of darkness over the entire countryside, and Raymond came to the decision that enough was enough—he was going back to bed. He had got up, stretched, and was about to step out into the open, when the sound of approaching foot-treads made him sink down again. With a pounding heart he listened to the heavy "crunch crunch", the snap of breaking wood, the crash of a bush being flattened, the swish of pliant branches pushed to one side, and knew—with an awful, unquestionable certainty—that the Mudadora, be it man, beast or monster, was coming in his direction.

Possibly never had a boy so regretted giving in to a mad impulse, as did Raymond, while crouched down behind his meagre bush. The thudding tread drew nearer, small life squealed and scurried through the undergrowth, birds awakened either by sound or pure instinct, twittered with alarm and rose up from nearby trees and became whirling shapes that could just be seen in the dim light.

Raymond, trembling, not knowing if he should stay where he was or run for the house, peered with fearful expectancy into the gloom and waited for horror to come out from the trees. Then a fallen branch snapped, a pine-cone that had been kicked by a massive foot came rolling under the bush—and a black shape loomed up against the cloud-racked sky.

Raymond became aware of an overwhelming smell of dank earth, rotting vegetation, plus a cloying sweet odour, and he knew it was no mere wild animal that stood a few metres away, but something that had been born from corruption. But it was still too dark for him to see more than a bare outline; a round blob of a head, the bulk of hunched shoulders, a ragged covering that might have been fur, which in places glimmered with a green, luminous light. Then a flash of lightning momentarily turned night into day, and Raymond was quite unable to smother a cry of terror when he at last saw the tall, thickset figure from which tiny twigs jutted out from glutinous mud, sprouting here and there into clumps of wild plants that somehow had taken root in this walking lump of tainted earth. The head came round, and green, glittering eyes glared in Raymond's direction, while that bubbling cough grew into a terrible roar of anticipation. As though in answer, a crash of thunder made the night tremble, went echoing across the shrouded heavens, then sank down into an angry rumbling before dying away.

The Mudadora took one step towards Raymond's hiding-place—then another—and Raymond jumped to his feet, looked anxiously from left to right, then ran towards the house.

He should have reached it without any great difficulty, for the Mudadora was a clumsy creature, only able to move with slow, ponderous steps. But in the darkness he did not see the patch of brambles that hid an ant-hill, and suddenly he was on the ground, held fast by a tangle of thorn-covered stems. Another flash of lightning made every tree, bush, blade of grass stand out in stark relief, and revealed the Mudadora advancing towards him, black, fibre-covered arms outstretched, its mouth a green, yawning cavern, its eyes gleaming like starlit emeralds.

Raymond cried out: "Grandfather ... help me ... help me ..."

Another peal of thunder mingled with the monster's roar, shattered the darkness into slabs of terror-haunted nightmare, and completely smothered Raymond's shrill cry. He struggled and came up from the ground with torn clothes and scratched hands. Lightning flashes followed one after the other, and the mud-born creature was now only a couple of metres away, its body a shimmering, green mass that flattened hope with every step. Fear paralysed Raymond's legs, and he could not run, or even move, just stand there and wait for an unthinkable end.

The great arms were raised, curved down towards the boy's trembling shoulders. Then, suddenly, the rains came.

All at once, a veritable deluge poured down from the black, seething sky; thudded on ground and forest roof, cascaded from battered leaves and over-filled gutters—and made the Mudadora cringe as though in abject terror.

It turned and began to lumber back towards the forest, emitting a low, bubbling cry as rain teemed down over its head, sent cold watery spears into its shoulders, flailing arms and slowly moving legs. Raymond knew it was trying to reach the trees, where a certain amount of shelter could provide protection from this sudden cloud-burst which was gradually washing away the life-preserving mud.

With fear-inspired desperation he tore his feet free from the brambles and performed the most courageous act of his entire life. He ran forward and crashed into the back of the reeling monster. It fell to the ground with a soggy thud and lay there, struggling feebly, while rain seeped into the flickering eyes, gaping mouth; tore holes in the luminous face and glistening body.

25

Then he heard his grandfather's voice calling from his bedroom window: "Raymond ... where are you?" before he too slumped down on to the drenched earth and lay still.

Sunlight had transformed his bedroom into a golden grotto when Raymond came back into the world of the living, and, for a while, he could not remember what had taken place. He lay quite still and looked up at the ceiling and was thinking it must be long past his normal hour for getting up, when a single word slid into his brain.

"Mudadora."

He sat up in bed and became aware that his grandfather was seated on a chair beside him. The old man creased his face into a smile and gave a vast sigh of relief.

"Thank goodness! I was wondering if I should not go down to the village and bring back the doctor. How do you feel?"

"What about the ... Mudadora?"

Mr Carstairs cast an anxious glance at the closed door.

"Not so loud, my boy. Your grandmother—she mustn't know anything about—you know what. She would worry herself ill. Suffice to say that due to your courageous action, the—the creature was almost dead when I carried you back into the house. The heavy rain washed the skeleton clean. I buried it in the forest this morning. Your grandmother thinks you walked in your sleep, and you must never tell her what really happened."

Raymond promised he would keep the story to himself, but was quite unable to retain his curiosity.

"But why wasn't it washed away by the rain long ago?"

Mr Carstairs shrugged. "I can only guess, altnougn our friend Jasper can probably give you a more detailed answer. Its entire existence was spent deep in the forest, where the large trees would provide cover and no doubt it had a den of some kind, possibly a cave or a hole in the ground. You lured it out into the open, and the unusually heavy downpour caught it completely unawares."

Later, Raymond, a little the worse for his adventure, went downstairs, where his grandmother gave him an enormous breakfast and said he must never, never walk in his sleep again. But when he again accompanied his grandfather for a walk through the forest, and they both told Jasper of how the Mudadora came to its watery end, the little man smiled grimly and said: "So, it walks no more! But the forest still lives, and there be other things that crawl, slither and wriggle through the undergrowth. Aye, that there be."

THE SLIPPITY-SLOP

By Henry Glynn

Reginald liked digging holes.

Give him a spade, a patch of ground, and he was as happy as a mouse in a cheese shop. Understandably his father did not approve of this earth-disturbing occupation, which sometimes resulted in young plants being uprooted, aspiring potatoes left to perish under the noonday sun, and a general air of disarray in the garden.

"Look here," he protested, while looking ruefully down into a most respectable hole that had ruined his rhubarb crop. "This can't go on. If you must dig holes, find a place that hasn't been cultivated."

"Where?" Reginald demanded, for he was a lad who did not waste words. He reserved his energy for digging.

"Oh," his father looked helplessly round the garden. "Over there in the corner. Nothing will grow there, not even weeds."

The patch of ground in question was about two metres square, black as a chimney-sweep's face and always rather damp. Not exactly soggy, but moist, inclined to squelch if one jumped on it—which, of course, Reginald did at irregular intervals—and not really a one hundred per cent digging place. But he was not a boy to look a gift horse in the mouth—whatever that may mean—and lost no time in pushing his spade into the dank soil and depositing a glutinous clod on to the newly laid gravel path.

There was no doubt that the hole—if I may be permitted the expression—was most reluctant to be dug.

The sides fell in and covered his legs with thick, horribly clinging soil; great fat, slimy worms slithered round his spade, and there was a distinct feeling that he was not so much digging a hole as burying himself.

But Reginald persevered, shovelled out just a little more than fell in, and, after a lot of back-breaking work, was rewarded by seeing a respectable heap above, and something that bore a reasonable resemblance to a hole below. Then his spade struck a hard surface and he was forced to stop and investigate.

It was a round slab of stone.

Five minutes later a very muddy, irritated Reginald approached his father, who had just filled in the rhubarb-patch hole and was in no mood to discuss further spadework activities. He gave his young son one horrified glance, then raised his voice in protest.

"Good grief! Look at you! What on earth your mother is going to say, I can't think."

"Stone in hole," Reginald stated. "Can't move it."

"Never mind stones in holes. Inside this instant . . ."

"Got writing on it," Reginald interrupted. "Can't read it."

Mr Straddlegrass, for such I must admit was Reginald's father's name, was clearly interested by this latest scrap of information, for he closed his mouth, gave the impression that he might well be thinking, then said: "Writing you say! On a slab of stone? Let's have a look."

Naturally the pile of earth on the garden-path aroused adverse comment, particularly as it had spilt over on to a bed of prize dahlias, but this was forgotten—if not forgiven—when Mr Straddlegrass looked down into the gaping hole.

"What a ghastly-looking mess! And all those worms! Ugh!"

"Dirt fallen on stone," Reginald pointed out

"So I can see. Well, I suppose I'd better go down there. You stay here."

He slid down into the hole and began to push the loose earth to one side with the toe of his shoe.

"You're right, there is a stone here. And bless my breeches if there aren't some letters etched on it."

"That's what I said," Reginald insisted.

"I know you did. There's no need to be so cheeky. Hand me the spade."

The spade made a grating sound as it scraped over stone, then Mr Straddlegrass spoke again, but this time his voice carried an undertone of excitement.

"Throw me down a piece of stick or something. The letters are filled with earth."

Reginald passed down a length of bamboo which had been supporting a dahlia, then waited with ill-concealed impatience for further developments. Actually he was not in the least interested as to what was written on the stone, only in having it speedily removed so he could continue enlarging his hole. Presently his father began to spell out words, but with great difficulty.

"Dis-turb not that which lies be-neath,
Or you'll run home with chat-tering teeth.
It mat-ters not if you bolt door;
For Slip-pity-Slop come up through floor."

Reginald was not very impressed with this piece of doggerel and quickly got back to the essential problem.

"Can you get stone up now?"

His father clambered out of the hole, then scratched his head.

" 'Disturb not that which lies beneath!' I wonder if there's anything down there?"

"Get stone up and find out," Reginald continued to stress his point.

30

"Don't suppose there's anything worth having," Mr Straddlegrass said. "But you never know. Might be treasure or something."

Reginald considered this to be extremely unlikely, but was prepared to encourage any project, no matter how far-fetched, that would ensure the impediment to his hole-digging was removed.

"Bound to be treasure. Get stone up now."

His father appeared to give the matter his full attention for an entire minute, then nodded vigorously.

"I believe I will. Can't do any harm."

Reginald, without further waste of words, handed him the spade. There followed a period of scraping, earth-loosening, heaving, much use of strange words, and finally, a mighty rending sound. Mr Straddlegrass lifted the slab of stone and, with great effort, tossed it on to the path.

"Now," he said, wiping his hands on the legs of his trousers, "let's see what's down there."

Reginald would have pointed out that he was quite willing to carry on with the good work, but decided that his father was entitled to a well-earned treat after all that stone-raising. So he sat down on the pile of earth and watched his perspiring parent wield a spade with more energy than skill. Presently Mr Straddlegrass made a sound that was a blend of "Ugh" and "Ah" and threw something out of the hole. The object rolled along the garden-path and finished up between two rows of runner beans.

It looked like a large black egg—with roots. Oval-shaped, pitted, still covered with moist soil, it was more than half a metre long and possibly fifty centimetres in circumference. The roots were slightly pink and sprouted from one side. Mr Straddlegrass examined this unexpected piece of treasure with interest.

31

"Horrible-looking thing," he observed. "But un-usual. I wonder if it's worth anything?"

So far as Reginald was concerned, he would not have paid three pence for it, but he knew adults often gave large sums for the most unlikely things.

"How much?" he enquired, while looking at the egg-shaped object with marked distaste.

His father shrugged. "Depends what it is. There might be some collector who's got a fancy for such things, willing to pay quite a price. I mean to say, how often do you see an egg with roots?"

Reginald had to admit this was a rare commodity, although he personally could jog along quite happily without one on the mantelpiece. He pushed the thing with his foot and thereby earned a rebuke from his father.

"Hey, watch it! That shell don't look all that thick and if it gets cracked, then no one will pay anything for it." He cast an apprehensive look at the kitchen window. "I suppose we had better show it to your mother."

"I don't like the look of it and that's a fact," Mrs Straddlegrass protested. "It looks horrible, it smells horrible and I'm sure it *is* horrible."

"But it is very rare," Mr Straddlegrass pointed out. "And rare things are always valuable."

"Well, take it somewhere else. I don't want it in my kitchen. I wouldn't be happy washing up, knowing that thing was right next to my feet."

Reginald had to admit that the egg-shaped object had improved after a good wash under the cold tap. It now had a kind of reddish surface, which, although pitted, was rather pretty, if one did not look at it for too long. The roots, of course—which had not taken kindly to the hasty shampoo—rather created the impression that a number of very thin legs had become entangled, but, given time, would sort themselves out and come running across the floor.

"Where can I put it?" Mr Straddlegrass insisted.

"Dustbin."

Reginald shook his head reprovingly at this example of adult bickering, and said: "Loft. No one go up there."

His mother smiled and ruffled his hair. "That's a very sensible suggestion. Apart from the dustbin, that's the best place for it. But make sure you shut the trapdoor."

"But it's very hot up there," Mr Straddlegrass objected. "It might—well—go bad."

"It can't be badder than it is. That's my last word on the subject. Loft or dustbin. Take your choice."

The egg-shaped object was put up into the loft, where it nestled between an old wellington boot and a pile of magazines. Mr Straddlegrass placed an advertisement in the local newspaper, which stated he had a large black egg with roots for sale, but no one seemed interested. In fact, there was not one single reply.

"I tell you there are rats in the loft," Mrs Straddlegrass insisted. "I distinctly heard a slithering sound."

"Impossible." Her husband rarely answered back, but on this occasion he felt certain he was on safe ground. "Rats can't get up into the loft. I can't myself, for that matter. The trapdoor's jammed. Anyway, rats don't slither. They patter."

Mrs Straddlegrass shook her head. "No pattering. These slither."

"Birds?" Mr Straddlegrass suggested.

Reginald thought it was about time he aired his knowledge.

"Birds twitter."

His mother looked upon him with all the pride natural to a lady who has raised a genius, then shot her husband a withering glance. "There now, at nine years

33

of age he's got more sense in his little finger than you have in your entire body."

Mr Straddlegrass sighed deeply. "Well, anyway, it can't be rats. If you want my opinion, there's nothing up there. Imagination."

Reginald decided the conversation had become a little boring, for personally he could not care less if something in the loft slithered, twittered or pattered. So he went into the garden, which was disgustingly neat, with not a single hole to enliven its rows of sprouting potatoes, feathery carrots, flourishing cabbages and other plant life, that were a source of pride to Mr Straddlegrass. Even the damp patch which had former- ly contained the egg-shaped object was covered by an elaborate rockery.

Reginald added his contribution by throwing a stone on the rockery then turned about and looked idly back at the house, It was bright with new paint and gleaming windows and appeared to be smirking at him, as though it knew something that he did not and had no intention of revealing the secret. He muttered: "Rotten house. Rotten garden. Rotten everything."

Then he spotted something move behind a chimney-stack, and life took on a fresh glow of interest again. At first he thought a large bird had set up home in a chimney-pot, and waited for it to reappear. But after the first flurry of movement, which he had only seen from the corner of one eye, the roof continued to present a normal, innocent appearance; a grey slope of smooth slates, surmounted by four red chimney-pots.

He was about to walk back along the path, for his mother usually made a cup of cocoa at this time, when a great, round head reared up from behind the chimney-stack. It looked like a big soup-plate, equipped with eyes and a pair of tapering ears. So far as Reginald could see, this terrifying head was supported by a long, scale-

34

covered neck, which wrinkled whenever the creature swayed from left to right. Having—so to speak—taken the air, it sank down and presumably disappeared through a hole in the roof.

Reginald ran down the path, fired by a quite natural urge to inform his parents about this disturbing tenant who had taken up residence in their loft.

"Ah, there you are!" Mrs Straddlegrass greeted him. "Just in time for a nice cup of cocoa and a condensed-milk sandwich."

"Big head looking over chimney," Reginald imparted the news with his accustomed economy of words.

"Yes, dear. And I'm sure it's a very nice head. Now sit down."

"Wrinkled neck," Reginald added. "Face like soup-plate."

"I think," Mr. Straddlegrass stated, "I'll dig up some of them 'taters. Be very nice boiled and served up with a bit of roast lamb."

"Egg must have hatched out," Reginald insisted, knowing he must be very patient, as adult brains do not absorb information very quickly. "Slippity-Slop grown up."

His mother beamed. "Isn't he a one! My dad had a wonderful imagination. After three pints of beer he said my mother had three heads and more arms that she knew what to do with."

Mr Straddlegrass nodded grimly. "She had plenty of mouth at any rate."

"And," Reginald continued, "it slithers in loft."

If I may be permitted to use a hackneyed phrase—the penny finally dropped. Both parents looked upon their offspring with growing interest. It was Mr Straddlegrass who broke the rather disturbing silence. "What did you say, son?"

"Slippity-Slop hatched out. Grown big. Made hole in roof. Slithering."

Father looked at mother, both turned pale, then exchanged words of disbelief.

"He's having us on!"

"It's just not possible."

Reginald sighed and wondered—not for the first time—how such a stupid pair had managed to produce an intelligent being like himself.

"Easy to make sure. Open trap door and look."

There seemed to be a marked reluctance to carry out this excellent advice. Mr Straddlegrass shifted uneasily in his chair, and Mrs Straddlegrass took a deep swig of cocoa from an extremely large mug. At length she said: "Can't do any harm—can it?"

Her husband agreed it could not, but continued to sit in his chair and stare thoughtfully at the floor. Then Reginald, who was becoming a little impatient with all this dithering, got to his feet.

"I'll get pair of steps."

"But the trapdoor is jammed, son."

"And hammer to unjam."

Such praiseworthy zeal was not greeted with the enthusiasm it deserved, for his mother said: "Drink your cocoa and don't be so forward," and his father made a funny face and looked sadly out of the window. After a while, Reginald decided that he would have to let time reveal that which no one wished to see, so he drank his cocoa, ate two condensed-milk sandwiches, then went out to play with the next-door cat, who liked nothing better than chasing a piece of string with a conker tied on one end.

When he came in for lunch, his father was laying the table, this being one of his many household duties, and wearing an expression of subdued optimism.

"Not a thing up there," he informed Reginald. "I've banged on the trapdoor, but it won't budge. But there was no sound, so there can't be anything up there."

"Sleeping. Need screwdriver to remove frame . . ."

"I've had enough of your suggestions. Now, get the pepper and salt out of the sideboard and don't talk so much."

In fact, no one spoke very much during lunch, except to say: "Any more sprouts?" and "That pudding is filling," and other mundane remarks. Then something made a loud thudding sound above stairs, and Mrs Straddlegrass said how careless Reginald was to leave things in places where they could fall down, and how Mr Straddlegrass should keep an eye on him, as she had only one pair of legs and couldn't be in every place at once. This was an injustice that Reginald could not tolerate, so, after he had eaten his second helping of treacle pudding, he said quietly: "Nothing fall down. Slippity-Slop wake up. Soon come down through ceiling."

Both parents told him to shut up and uttered dire threats about him being sent to bed without any supper, then jumped to their feet when a loud splintering sound, followed by a crash, appeared to confirm his prophecy. Reginald, who had a genuine thirst for knowledge and just could not understand this reluctance to face the unknown, got up and walked into the hall, then slowly mounted the stairs.

Most of the landing ceiling had crashed down on to the carpet, and from the midst of a mass of sagging lathes and splintered beams, a long, scaled neck, which was terminated by a large, soup-plate-shaped head, swayed back and forth like a giant, grotesque snake. The round, green eyes surveyed the intruder with a cold, malevolent stare, while the wide, well-fanged jaws crunched a lump of plaster. Then the remainder of the ceiling collapsed, and Reginald was able to view the monster in its entirety.

To say the least, it was an unnerving sight. Imagine a

A large soup-plate-shaped head swayed back and forth . . .

short, round body that tapered down to the neck on one side and a long, thin tail on the other. Then give the body sixteen pairs of legs, each one equipped with a green, sucker-like foot, that most certainly made an awful slithering sound as they slid among the fallen plaster. The creature seemed to be in no way put out by its fall, but reached out its long neck and took an experimental bite out of the bannisters.

Reginald went back downstairs and into the dining-room where he found his parents huddled under the table. He knelt down and did his best to comfort them.

"No need to worry. Slippity-Slop eating bannisters."

It is regretted that neither parent was reassured by this information or thanked Reginald for imparting it. Mrs Straddlegrass was the first to emerge and she proclaimed her fear and indignation in a loud voice.

"It's all your fault, digging holes and letting your father bring that egg-thing into the house. Well, I'm going to shut myself in the kitchen and not come out until one or both of you have found some way of getting rid of that awful creature."

Mr Straddlegrass clambered out from under the table.

"Of course, dear. I'll ring the police and fire brigade."

"No you don't. I'm not having the neighbours know we've a monster on the premises. It's not respectable."

And, having uttered these final words, the good lady departed, leaving a very frightened and perplexed Mr Straddlegrass staring hopefully at his completely un-moved son.

"Eh . . . what do you think we ought to do?"

Reginald nodded his approval. His father was at last showing a glimmer of intelligence, in so far as he was requesting advice from someone who thought before speaking.

"Hole," he said.

"You can't dig holes now. How are we going to get shot of that thing?"

Reginald sighed deeply. "Egg come from hole—Slippity-Slop go back down hole."

Mr Straddlegrass again gave the impression that he was thinking.

"Fine. But how do we get it down a hole?"

Reginald did not answer, but went out into the garden, where he half filled one jacket pocket with moist earth before returning to the house and motioning to an agitated parent.

"Upstairs," he ordered.

But Mr Straddlegrass needed a lot of persuasion before he could be prevailed upon to mount the stairs, and, even then, Reginald had to all but pull him up the last few steps. The Slippity-Slop had not found the bannisters to its liking and was now tackling the right-hand wall. It sucked, crunched, slipped and slopped; it consumed wallpaper and plaster at an alarming rate, then made a loud coughing sound when inadvertently swallowing a lump of loose brick.

"Not right food," Reginald explained to a trembling Mr Straddlegrass. "Get indigestion."

He took a handful of soil from his pocket, spread it out on that part of the bannister rail that was still intact, then stood back to await developments. The Slippity-Slop stopped munching, turned its head, and stared at this offering with unblinking eyes. Presently the long neck came down, a black tongue flicked out and the soil disappeared, together with a thin sliver of wood. The monster then gave vent to a high-pitched cry before sniffing the bannisters with keen expectancy. Reginald addressed his bulging-eyed father.

"Earth natural food. Must spread some on stairs all the way to hall."

40

"Must we?" Mr Straddlegrass whispered. "Suppose it tries to eat us?"

"Wants to eat dirt. Sort of big worm."

And without wasting any more words, Reginald ran down the stairs and out into the garden, where he grabbed a spade and began to dig a really first-class hole in the middle of the cabbage-patch. It says much for Mr Straddlegrass's state of mind that he did not so much as flinch when fat cabbages were tossed to one side, while his son piled up earth with professional skill, going deeper and deeper, until only his head was above ground. Then he climbed up on to the path and began to fill his mother's washing basket with damp soil.

"I don't mind giving you a hand," Mr Straddlegrass volunteered. "So long as I don't have to go more than halfway up the stairs."

In fact, neither had to ascend more than six steps, for the moment the Slippity-Slop detected a whiff of its natural food, it came slithering down the stairs, smashing bannisters and tearing up the carpet in the process. Of course, Mr Straddlegrass took to his heels, and Reginald had to drag the basket down into the hall, jerking it back whenever the monster tried to bury its head in the soil, while trying to ignore his mother's voice which kept demanding to know what was going on.

Eventually he reached the garden, pulled the basket over the back doorstep, down the path, and finally to his recently dug hole. He straightened up and pointed to the deep cavity.

"Food," he said.

The Slippity-Slop advanced very slowly, as though not believing that such a splendid supply of natural nourishment actually existed. It sniffed at a few cabbages, sucked up a few parsnips, sampled some of the earth, then looked down into the hole.

Reginald watched this large, fearsome creature and,

41

for the first time, wondered how the egg-shaped object had come to be buried in their garden. Or had it been planted? Was the Slippity-Slop a cross between a plant and animal; the result of some strange experiment performed in a bygone age? Perhaps there had been others which had died or been destroyed, and the last egg—seed—had been buried under a stone, as though the unknown scientist was unable to completely destroy his own work, but could not again face a fully grown monster.

One thing was certain—the Slippity-Slop fully approved of large holes. The soup-plate-shaped head sucked up the loose soil which lay at the bottom, then wriggled into some more—and more—all the while going deeper and deeper, until the long neck was completely hidden. Then the round body slid over the edge and sank down into the agitated earth, disappearing from view. Finally there was only the very tip of the tail, waving away like a small worm that had come up to sample the evening air.

Suddenly the entire hole trembled as though disturbed by a minor earthquake; the sides fell in, and a shuddering crack went streaking across the garden. The Slippity-Slop was burrowing a passage to places unknown. Reginald took a deep breath. "Now I'll fill in rest of hole."

Which was the first time he had ever volunteered to do anything like that.

I am certain the Slippity-Slop is still alive and slithering. Also, for all I know, it has laid eggs—or shed seeds—and there may well be hundreds of these ugly creatures wriggling around under your feet. So, take my advice—never dig a hole unless it is absolutely necessary. Should you uncover a stone slab with an inscription engraved on it, shovel the earth back in again as quickly as you can.

42

And finally—if an egg-shaped object with roots should turn up, don't put it in the loft. Wrap it up in brown paper and post it to someone you don't like. Or send it to the Natural History Museum. It might look well in the prehistoric-monster section.

LEGEND OF THE SPIDERS

By Keith Timsom

"It is a grim tale," the chieftain declared, "and not for the ears of someone who is so young."

"I don't mind," Tony enthused. "The gorier the better!"

The chieftain seemed unconvinced and looked in the direction of the boy's father, to seek approval. For a moment there was an awful silence.

"Tony is only a young lad, but he is the son of a space ambassador," the father mused. "He has got to learn sooner or later that a lot of nasty things happen in this galaxy of ours. Perhaps . . ."

He was interrupted by the sound of something smashing its way through the jungle. A gigantic, hairy leg burst out from the undergrowth, then another, and another.

"Keep down," the chieftain ordered, as they stared up at a huge brown underbelly.

Daylight appeared again, and the sound of more foliage being crushed, before they were able to continue.

"I could not see who was responsible," the old chieftain with the silver beard grunted. "But I promise you that when I find out, I shall let that person hear the rough edge of my tongue."

"Never mind," Tony's father consoled. "None of us came to any harm and that is all that matters."

"It would have mattered a long time ago."

"Would it?" Tony asked, seizing upon the opportunity of hearing the chieftain's gory tale.

44

"I can see that you are determined to hear the Legend of the Spiders. If I do not tell you, then I expect that someone else will during one of your future visits."

"That is true enough," the boy's father added. "Tony is not a squeamish lad, as he has just proved. Let him hear the tale before we leave."

"It goes right back to the beginning," the chieftain announced, as he started to unfold his story. "To when our tribe was afraid to live in the jungle."

Tony crossed his legs and propped his elbows on his knees, just as he always did when he knew that he was going to listen to or watch something that might turn out to be exciting.

"The name of our hero is Chan, and he lived on the other side of the planet; the barren part which is more than a desert. Chan and his friend Lanta were the very first to brave the creatures of these lands, and even they did not do it by choice."

"Why not?" Tony interrupted. "It's such a wonderful place."

"Because, my young friend, we did not have the services of our greatest ally in those days. However, you rush me. This tale happened a long time ago, when Chan and Lanta were mere slaves of the Samals."

"The Samals?"

"Yes, the Samals. A fearful race of people who attacked our tribe, killing many, and enslaving those who were useful to them. Chan and Lanta were two of the luckier ones.

"One day they managed to escape. There was only one place too which their captors would not follow them—and that was the jungle. They ran as fast as they could, miraculously escaping the clutches of the pursuing Samals, who only gave up the chase when they reached the edge of the trees.

" 'You will die a far worse death in there,' " Vana, the

45

chief Samal mocked, 'than, by any torture that we could have invented.'

" 'Goodbye, Vana,' Chan replied, as arrows rained down about him. 'One day I shall return.'

"He heard them laugh as he joined his friend Lanta in the comparative safety of the undergrowth.

" 'I would rather die in this place than at the hands of the Samals,' Lanta muttered.

" 'We shall not die, Lanta,' Chan said comfortingly. 'Here, take some of the fruits from this tree.'

"They ate, both of them secretly afraid that the berries might be poisonous. Fortunately they were not, and, once they had eaten, they fell asleep.

"Chan was awakened by something that had clamped around his stomach. It lifted him high into the air. As he opened his eyes, he realised that he and Lanta were being carried in the claws of a gigantic, hairy spider.

"He struggled to free himself, knowing that the monster's massive legs were carrying them to its lair. But it was no use. The monster forced them through the thick foliage of the jungle. Terror struck, Chan knew that he and his companion had no choice but to contemplate a death which would be far worse than anything that the Samals could have conceived.

" 'Pray, Lanta,' he said, as the claws tightened. 'The end has come.'

"The last branch snapped against them as they came to a clearing with a large open hollow in its centre. Clearly, this was to be the scene of their deaths, but why had the spider dug itself a lair that was so open and exposed? It was obvious that it feared no other creature."

"Gosh!" Tony interupted again. "Fancy thinking about something like that when you are about to be eaten alive!"

46

"That was why he was such a special man," his father added. "Remember, this is his story."

"What happened next is not for the squeamish," the chieftain continued. "The time had come   they were now in the hollow.

"But Chan had a sudden reprieve, for the claw which held him, opened up, and he fell to the ground. He picked himself up and powerlessly watched his friend die.

"It is written that brave Lanta did not even scream as he was lowered towards the spider's gaping jaws. Mercifully his head was bitten clean off, first of all before the monster gorged upon the rest of his body, leaving only the largest bones.

"Blood dripped from its mouth as it stared down at its next victim. Chan braced himself and stared defiantly back into the hideous face. Then he realised that his death was to come later, for two hairy lids were starting to close over the spider's malevolent black eyes. It was soon asleep.

"Most men would have gone mad, just sitting there, as Chan did, amongst the rotting bones, the stench of dried blood filling his nostrils and with nothing to do but imagine what being eaten by a man-eating spider was really going to be like. But Chan was different to other men. While he was alive, he knew that he still had a chance. I hope that you are never in such a situation, Tony. But if you are, then remember that while you are still alive, all is not lost."

The chieftain continued his story.

"The hollow was a perfectly shaped, deep bowl, from which there seemed no escape. Even if it was possible to scale the sides, the time that Chan would need was probably longer than the spider's nap.

"Yet Chan refused to admit that he was beaten. He owed it to the memory of his friend to die fighting. He

47

Lanta was lowered towards the spider's gaping jaws . . .

walked beneath the shadow of the spider's legs, which towered above him like huge, hairy trees. The snores of the monster deafened him as they bellowed around the hollow. It was then that the idea came to him."

"I think I can guess what it was," Tony interrupted yet again. "He did have a chance, didn't he?"

"Yes, he did. For he had suddenly realised that there was something which a two-legged creature could do, that none of the monster's four-legged victims were capable of. But he realised that his timing would have to be perfect, as he looked at the gaps between the creature's front legs and the claws on either side.

"Chan chose the right side, praying that he had not been weakened too much by the chase across the desert. As he stood against the side of the hollow, preparing to take as long a run as possible, he reminded himself that failure to land on the back of the spider's neck would mean only one thing, for, by now, it must have been hungry again.

"He ran as fast as he could and leapt high into the air. His shoulder jarred against one of its legs. The monster stirred.

"Desperately, Chan grabbed the long hairs on the top of its head. He kicked with both legs, praying that they would carry him over. They did.

"He was now astride the creature's neck, and able to stretch his arms around the throat, hoping that he might be able to throttle the beast. But the larynx was too well protected by a thick layer of skin, and there was no other weapon to use, besides his bare hands.

"The spider tossed its head from side to side, and almost succeeded in hurling Chan back on to the ground. It was obvious that it was just as determined to rid itself of its passenger as Chan was to become its rider.

"Suddenly, without warning, it bounded out of the

hollow and dashed into the jungle. Branches smashed against Chan, even though he tried to bury himself amongst the musty-smelling hairs on the monster's head.

"They came to a deep gorge. The spider scampered down one of the steep sides and up the other, yet Chan still managed to hold on.

"It was a long time before the spider started to tire. Chan grabbed bunches of berries from the trees as they passed beneath them, knowing that he needed plenty of food to sustain him, for the creature was not going to give up the struggle yet.

"They passed out of the jungle and came to the fields that surrounded the mountains. Suddenly the monster collapsed to the ground and was very soon asleep again.

"Now was Chan's chance to escape. Perhaps that is what the spider wanted, having now come to terms with the fact that Chan was the one victim that had got away. Our hero was no doubt tempted, but he remained on the monster's back."

Tony again interrupted.

"If he had wanted to, he could even have climbed down and found something to kill it with."

"Yes, Tony, he could even have done that, but he did not. Chan was a man of vision: the whole future rested upon the conquest of this king of the jungle.

"The spider did not sleep for long. There would now be the great test of all; Chan knew exactly what his enemy was intending to do. Before them was Tara, the highest mountain on our planet. If he survived the challenge, then Chan would have mastered the spider.

"Once more ready for battle, the monster deliberately chose the sheer, at times vertical, face on the northern side, to reach the summit of the mountain. It climbed higher and higher, as Chan clung desperately to the thick hairs, his legs dangling, unable to grip upon its body at such an angle.

"When the monster reached the top of the mountain, it immediately bolted down the other side with the speed of a snake. This was an even more terrible ordeal than the journey upwards. Chan was tossed and buffeted as it scrambled over the rocks, and on many occasions almost pitched over the spider's head, to what would have been certain death on the rocks below. Surely this was to be the final test?

"It was. The spider collapsed from exhaustion when it reached the bottom. Chan rested his aching body as best he could, yet still as determined to remain on the creature's back as he was before.

"He did not enjoy his rest for long. The spider decided to climb Tara all over again. However, this time it deliberately chose the easiest route. Chan had won."

"But why did it want to climb the mountain again?" Tony asked.

"Can't you guess?"

Tony thought hard, but could not think of the answer.

"The spider had realised that Chan was only able to jump on its back and avoid some of the heavy branches that it ran beneath in the jungle, because his eyesight was superior."

"You can see almost everything from the top of Tara," Tony said thoughtfully. "Chan would be its lookout. Is that it?"

"That is exactly it, my young friend," the old man continued. "From such a high vantage, it was possible to spot the whereabouts of any herds of animals which were grazing below.

"The system was simple. If Chan wanted to guide the creature to the left, then he would gently tap the left-hand side of its head. For the right, vice versa.

"For a long time, Chan actually lived on the back of the spider, only daring to leave it for a short while when it was asleep, and helping it to hunt when it was awake.

"He soon became the friend of all the other spiders, and, with his superior eyesight, was able to lead a whole pack on successful hunting forays.

"During all this time, Chan had conceived a plan which would rid his people of the tyranny of the Samals. Once he was confident that he had completely gained their trust, he led his new spider friends into the desert.

"The devious Samals did exactly as he expected. They fled for their lives, having left Chan's enslaved people trapped in a covered pit, in the hope that these monsters, which had appeared on the horizon, would feed themselves so well that they would not bother to pursue them. But the spiders did no such thing; as far as they were concerned, all humans were their friends.

"Chan uncovered the pit and helped his people climb out. When they saw the spiders, they were, quite naturally, terrified. It took a lot of effort to persuade them to actually jump on to their backs and ride upon them as he did.

"The rest of the story is the history of our people. These creatures became completely dependant upon us, especially when we used bows and arrows to hunt prey for them. Unfortunately, this combination proved so successful that all the other creatures were hunted out of existence. For a time it seemed that both men and spiders would perish, just as the Samals had done in the desert when they no longer had any slaves to work for them. Fortunately our tribe and their eight-legged friends were able to adapt themselves to the diet of a vegetarian. There have always been plenty of plants and fruits in the jungle, so, right up to the present time, we have all managed to survive."

"Is that why the spiders are so harmless now?" Tony asked.

"Yes, my little friend," the old chieftain confirmed. "The spiders are now completely domesticated."

"Just like the one which will carry us back to the ship," his father added. "It is time that we returned to Earth."

"Yes, and I must seek the fool who was riding that spider," the chieftain declared. "Peaceful they may be, but they still need careful handling."

"So it is goodbye for now," Tony's father said.

The chieftain stood up, and then bowed gracefully, as was their custom. Tony and his father returned this gesture and started to walk over to the spider, which had been patiently waiting for them.

"Young man!" the chieftain called out. "Remember that the spiders of today are totally dependant upon their owners and need constant grooming."

Tony stopped and grinned.

"I will," he promised. "And thanks for the story. I can't wait to tell it to my friends."

They climbed the small ladder at the side of the spider and sat themselves in the two comfortable seats that were secured to its neck. The ambassador patted its head, and they were soon being carried back to their spaceship.

"We'll be coming back before Christmas, won't we?" asked Tony.

"Yes, but why do you ask?"

"Would it be too much trouble to bring the transporter with us?"

"Oh, so that's it!"

"It could be a Christmas and birthday present combined. There are plenty of things that a spider could live on in the Amazon."

"We shall see."

Tony tried not to smile, for he knew that his father would eventually concede.

"Like the chieftain said," the ambassador mused with a twinkle in his eye, "they need a lot of grooming, and I know who is going to have to help to do that."

"It will be company for Mum when we are away."

"That's true."

Tony heard his father chuckle as he stroked the head of their mount. How his friends would envy him when he arrived at their home on the back of a giant spider!

THE PRINCE AND THE DRAGON

By Andrew Lang

ONCE upon a time there lived an emperor who had three sons. They were all fine young men, fond of hunting, and scarcely a day passed without one or other of them going out to look for game.

One morning, the eldest of the three princes mounted his horse and set out for a neighbouring forest, where wild animals of all sorts were to be found. He had not long left the castle when a hare sprang out of a thicket and dashed across the road in front of him. The young man gave chase at once and pursued it over hill and dale, till at last the hare took refuge in a mill which was standing by the side of a river.

The prince followed and entered the mill, but stopped in terror by the door, for, instead of a hare, before him stood a dragon, breathing fire and flame. At this fearful sight the prince turned to fly, but a fiery tongue coiled round his waist and drew him into the dragon's mouth, and he was seen no more.

A week passed by, and when the prince did not come back, everyone in the town began to grow uneasy. At last his next brother told the emperor that he likewise would go out to hunt, and perhaps would find some clue to his brother's disappearance. But hardly had the castle gates closed on the prince, than the hare sprang out of the bushes as before and led the huntsman up hill and down dale, till they reached the mill. Into this the hare flew with the prince at his heels, and lo, instead of the hare, there stood a dragon breathing fire and flame! Out shot a fiery tongue which coiled round the prince's waist and lifted him straight into the dragon's mouth, and he was seen no more.

Days went by, and the emperor waited and waited for the sons who did not return. He could not sleep at night for wondering where they were and what had become of them. His youngest son wished to go in search of his brothers, but for a long time the emperor refused to listen to him, lest he should lose him also. But the prince prayed so hard for leave to make the search, and promised so often that he would be very cautious and careful, that at length the emperor gave him permission and ordered the best horse in the stables to be saddled for him.

Full of hope, the young prince started on his way. But no sooner was he outside the city walls than a hare sprang out of the bushes and ran before him till they reached the mill. As before, the animal dashed in through the open door, but this time he was not followed by the prince.

Wiser than his brothers, the young man turned away, saying to himself, "There are as good hares in the forest as any that have come out of it, and, when I have caught them, I can come back and look for you."

For many hours he rode up and down the mountain, but saw nothing, and at last, tired of waiting, he went back to the mill. Here he found an old woman sitting, whom he greeted pleasantly.

"Good morrow to you, little mother," he said.

The old woman answered: "Good morrow, my son."

"Tell me, little mother," went on the prince, "where shall I find my hare?"

"My son," replied the old woman, "that was no hare, but a dragon who has led many men hither and then has eaten them all."

At these words the prince's heart grew heavy, and he

cried: "Then my brothers must have come here and have been eaten by the dragon!"

"You have guessed right," answered the old woman. "And I can give you no better counsel than to go home at once, before the same fate overtakes you."

"Will you not come with me out of this dreadful place?" said the young man.

"He took me prisoner, too," answered she, "and I cannot shake off his chains."

"Then listen to me," cried the prince. "When the dragon comes back, ask him where he always goes when he leaves here, and what makes him so strong? When you have coaxed the secret from him, tell me the next time I come."

So the prince went home, and the old woman remained in the mill. As soon as the dragon returned, she said to him: "Where have you been all this time—you have travelled far?"

"Yes, little mother, I have indeed travelled far," answered the dragon.

Then the old woman began to flatter him and to praise his cleverness. When she thought she had him in a good temper, she said: "I have wondered where you get your strength from; I do wish you would tell me. I would stoop and kiss the place out of pure love!"

The dragon laughed at this, and answered: "In the hearthstone yonder lies the secret of my strength."

Then the old woman jumped up and kissed the hearth, whereupon the dragon laughed the more, and said: "You foolish creature! I was only jesting. Is is not in the hearthstone, but in that tall tree that the secret of my strength lies."

The old woman jumped up again and put her arms round the tree, and kissed it heartily. Loudly laughed the dragon when he saw what she was doing.

"Old fool!" he cried, as soon as he could speak, "did

you really believe that my strength came from that tree?"

"Where is it then?" asked the old woman, rather crossly, for she did not like being made fun of.

"My strength," replied the dragon, "lies far away. So far that you could never reach it. Far, far from here is a kingdom, and by its capital city is a lake, and in the lake is a dragon, and inside the dragon is a wild boar, and inside the wild boar is a pigeon, and inside the pigeon a sparrow, and inside the sparrow is my strength."

When the old woman heard this, she thought it was no use flattering him any longer, for never, never, could she take his strength from him.

The following morning, when the dragon had left the mill, the prince came back, and the old woman told him all that the creature had said. He listened in silence and then returned to the castle, where he put on shepherd's clothes and, taking a staff in his hand, went forth to seek a place as a tender of sheep.

For some time he wandered from village to village and from town to town, till he came at length to a large city in a distant kingdom, surrounded on three sides by a great lake, which happened to be the very lake in which the dragon lived. As was his custom, the prince stopped everybody he met in the streets who looked likely to want a shepherd and begged them to engage him. But they all seemed to have shepherds of their own, or else not to need any. The prince was beginning to lose heart when a man, who had overheard his question, turned round and said that he had better go and ask the emperor, who was in search of someone to see after his flocks.

"Will you take care of my sheep?" asked the emperor, when the young man knelt before him.

"Most willingly, Your Majesty," answered the young man, and he listened obediently while the emperor told him what he was to do.

"Outside the city walls," said the emperor, "you will find a large lake; by its banks lie the richest meadows in my kingdom. When you are leading out your flocks to pasture, they will run straight to these meadows, and none that have gone there have ever been known to come back. Take heed, therefore, not to suffer your sheep to go where they will, but drive them to any spot you think best."

With a low bow, the prince thanked the emperor for his warning and promised to do his best to keep the sheep safe. Then he left the palace and went to the marketplace, where he bought two greyhounds, a hawk, and a set of pipes; after that he took the sheep out to pasture. The instant the animals caught sight of the lake lying before them, they trotted off as fast as their legs would go, to the green meadows lying round it.

The prince did not try to stop them; he placed his hawk on the branch of a tree, laid his pipes on the grass, and bade the greyhounds sit still. Then, rolling up his sleeves and trousers, he waded into the water, crying as he did so: "Dragon! Dragon! if you are not a coward, come out and fight with me!"

And a voice answered from the depths of the lake: "I am waiting for you, O Prince." The next minute, the dragon reared himself out of the water, huge and horrible to see. The prince sprang upon him, and they grappled with each other and fought together till the sun was high and it was noonday.

Then the dragon gasped: "O Prince, let me dip my burning head once into the lake and I will hurl you up to the top of the sky."

But the prince answered: "Oh, ho, my good dragon! Do not crow too soon! If the emperor's daughter were only here, and would kiss me on the forehead, I would throw you up higher still." And suddenly the dragon's hold loosened, and he fell back into the lake.

The dragon reared himself out of the water . . .

As soon as it was evening, the prince washed away all signs of the fight. He took his hawk upon his shoulder, his pipes under his arm, and, with his greyhounds in front and his flock following after him, he set out for the city. As they all passed through the streets, the people stared in wonder, for never before had any flock returned from the lake.

The next morning, the prince rose early and led his sheep down the road to the lake. This time, however, the emperor sent two men on horseback to ride behind him, with orders to watch the prince all day long. The horsemen kept the prince and his sheep in sight, without being seen themselves. As soon as they beheld the sheep running toward the meadows, they turned aside up a steep hill which overhung the lake. When the shepherd reached the place, he laid his pipes on the grass as before and bade the greyhounds sit beside them, while the hawk he perched on the branch of the tree.

Then he rolled up his trousers and his sleeves and waded into the water crying: "Dragon! Dragon! If you are not a coward, come out and fight with me!"

And the dragon answered: "I am waiting for you, O Prince," and the next minute he reared himself out of the water, huge and horrible to see. Again they clasped each other tight round the body and fought till it was noon, and, when the sun was at its hottest, the dragon gasped: " O Prince, let me dip my burning head once in the lake and I will hurl you up to the top of the sky."

But the prince answered, "Oh, ho! My good dragon, do not crow too soon! If the emperor's daughter were only here, and would kiss me on the forehead, I would throw you up higher still!"

And suddenly the dragon's hold loosened, and he fell back into the lake.

As soon as it was evening, the prince again collected
61

his sheep and, playing on his pipes, marched before them into the city. When he passed through the gates, all the people came out of their houses to stare in wonder, for never before had any flock returned from the lake.

Meanwhile the two horsemen had ridden quickly back, and told the emperor all that they had seen and heard. The emperor listened eagerly to their tale, then called his daughter to him and repeated it to her.

"Tomorrow," he said, when he had finished, "you shall go with the shepherd to the lake and then you shall kiss him on the forehead as he wishes."

When the princess heard these words, she burst into tears and sobbed out: "Will you really send me, your only child, to that dreadful place, from which most likely I shall never come back?"

"Fear nothing, my little daughter. All will be well. Many shepherds have gone to that lake and none have ever returned; but this one has, in these two days, fought twice with the dragon and has escaped without a wound. So I hope tomorrow he will kill the dragon and deliver this land from the monster who has slain so many of our bravest men."

Scarcely had the sun begun to peep over the hills next morning when the princess stood by the shepherd's side, ready to go to the lake. The shepherd was brimming over with joy, but the princess only wept bitterly.

"Dry your tears, I implore you," said he. "If you will just do what I ask you and, when the time comes, run and kiss my forehead, you have nothing to fear."

Merrily the shepherd blew on his pipes as he marched at the head of his flock, only stopping every now and then to say to the weeping girl at his side: "Do not cry so, Heart of Gold; trust me and fear nothing." And so they reached the lake.

In an instant, the sheep were scattered all over the

meadows and the prince placed his hawk on the tree and his pipes on the grass, while he bade his greyhounds lie beside them. Then he rolled up his trousers and his sleeves, and waded into the water, calling: "Dragon! Dragon! If you are not a coward, come forth and let us have one more fight together."

The dragon answered: "I am waiting for you, O Prince." And the next minute he reared himself out of the water, huge and horrible to see. Swiftly he drew near to the bank, and the prince sprang to meet him. They grasped each other round the body and fought till it was noon.

And when the sun was at its hottest, the dragon cried: "O Prince, let me dip my burning head in the lake and I will hurl you to the top of the sky."

But the prince answered: "Oh, ho! My good dragon, do not crow too soon! If the emperor's daughter were only here, and she would kiss my forehead, I would throw you higher still."

Hardly had he spoken when the princess, who had been listening, ran up and kissed him on the forehead. Then the prince swung the dragon straight up into the clouds, and, when he touched the earth again, he broke into a thousand pieces. Out of the pieces there sprang a wild boar which galloped away, but the prince called his hounds to give chase, and they caught the boar and tore it to bits. Out of the pieces there sprang a hare, and, in a moment, the greyhounds were after it, and they caught it and killed it; and out of the hare there came a pigeon. Quickly the prince let loose his hawk, which soared straight into the air, then swooped upon the bird, and brought it to his master. The prince cut open its body and found the sparrow inside, as the old woman had said.

"Now," cried the prince, holding the sparrow in his hand, "now you shall tell me where I can find my brothers."

"Do not hurt me," answered the sparrow, "and I will tell you with all my heart. Behind your father's castle stands a mill, and in the mill are three slender twigs. Cut off these twigs and strike their roots with them, and the iron door of a cellar will open. In the cellar you will find as many people, young and old, women and children, as would fill a kingdom, and among them are your brothers."

By this time twilight had fallen, so the prince washed himself in the lake, took the hawk on his shoulder and the pipes under his arm, and, with his greyhounds before him and his flock behind him, marched gaily into the town, the princess following them all, still trembling with fright. And so they passed through the streets, thronged with a wondering crowd, till they reached the castle.

Unknown to anyone, the emperor had stolen out on horseback and had hidden himself on the hill, where he could see all that happened. When all was over, and the power of the dragon was broken forever, he rode quickly back to the castle, and was ready to receive the prince with open arms and to promise him his daughter to wife.

The wedding took place with great splendour, and for a whole week the town was hung with coloured lamps, and tables were spread in the hall of the castle for all who chose to come and eat. And when the feast was over, the prince told the emperor and the people who he really was, and at this everyone rejoiced still more, and preparations were made for the prince and princess to return to their own kingdom, for the prince was impatient to set free his brothers.

The first thing he did when he reached his native country was to hasten to the mill, where he found the three twigs as the sparrow had told him. The moment that he struck the roots, the iron door flew open, and from the cellar a countless multitude of men and women streamed forth. He bade them go one by one wheresoever they would, while he himself waited by the door till his brothers passed through.

How delighted they were to meet again, and to hear all that the prince had done to deliver them from their enchantment. And they went home with him and served him all the days of their lives, for they said that he only who had proved himself brave and faithful was fit to be king.

THE BEAN ROCK MONSTER

By Terry Tapp

In the north-western region of Mexico, in the Gulf of California, the Rio Mayo slices through the rugged mountains of the Sierra Madre. This region is almost, but not quite, a desert; only the annual rains save it from becoming one. When those blessed rains do come, the most remarkable things imaginable happen.

Due to the arid conditions, few species of plants are able to thrive. Among those which do grow there are the giant cactus, oaks, thorn trees and the *yerba de flecha*.

My story concerns the *yerba de flecha*—so called because the local Mexican Indians used to dip their arrows in the milky-white sap of the plant to make them poisonous. The "plant of the arrows" is also remarkable because of its amazing beans.

Pablo Gonzalez lived in a village which was little more than a cluster of sun-baked mud huts. There were fifteen huts which were occupied by the villagers, and four extra huts which had been built to serve as a shelter for the animals, a food store, a church and a school. The village, too small to have a name, sheltered under the frowning brow of the Sierra Madre.

Every morning, Pablo would waken early in order to help his father, a leather-worker, before school time. He would sit cross-legged on the floor of the hut, slicing the left-over pieces of leather into fine strips, or polishing and embossing purses and wallets, which had been laboriously made by his father, ready for the monthly markets. Then, after a breakfast of pancakes and maple syrup, Pablo would run barefoot across the dusty compound to the school hut, where he would sit on his fibre mat and listen to Señor José Madello, the circuit teacher.

There were no excercise books in the tiny hut; just a blackboard leaning against the wall. Señor Madello would arrive promptly, count the heads of the children, then launch into his lesson immediately. After three hours of continuous work, he would leave the blackboard crammed with sums, or items for the children to learn. "When I come tomorrow," he would say, "I want you all to know these things." Then he would mount his rusty-coloured horse and race off to the next village.

One day, when the sun was so hot that the hut became almost unbearable, Señor Madello suggested that they should all climb up into the mountains and seek a cool spot where he could teach them. "I have something wonderful to show you," he said.

And so it was that eleven highly excited children followed the tall, copper-skinned teacher up the stumbling path into the bleached mountains in search of a cool morning breeze.

"We shall go to Bean Rock," he told them. "It is always nice and cool there in the mornings, and we shall collect the beans from the *yerba de flecha* so that I may explain them to you and tell you a story about them which is stranger than any fairy story you might read in a book. But remember, children, this is a true story. Sometimes the truth is stranger than things we make up."

"Why is it called Bean Rock, Señor?" asked Pablo.

"Have you not noticed that the rock looks exactly like a gigantic bean?" asked the teacher.

"Is it a giant bean?" Conchita, the youngest of the children, asked.

Señor Madello laughed and swept her up in his arms, for the journey was tiring for such a small girl.

"Well, no one really knows what Bean Rock is," he said. "Later this year we will have some very famous men coming to visit Bean Rock to try to tell us all about it. All we do know is that Bean Rock is radio-active and we should not stay too long near it."

"What is radio-active?" asked Conchita.

"Hard to explain," said the teacher. "Over there, miles into the desert, the scientists exploded an underground atomic bomb. For some years after that no one was allowed in this area. But now people are gradually returning to their homelands and building new villages and churches—and schools."

The children all gave a good-natured moan at that, and Señor Madello laughed. "You do not like school? I am shocked—quite shocked!" he said. But he was not at all.

Soon they arrived at Bean Rock and sat down in a circle around the teacher, enjoying the wafts of cool air.

"Bean Rock looks just like one of these," said Pablo, picking up a tiny bean from the ground.

"Indeed it does," agreed Señor Madello.

Suddenly Conchita shouted: "It moved! The bean moved!"

"That is why it is called the Mexican jumping bean," said the teacher.

"But *how* does it move?" asked Pablo. "It has no legs."

"Señor Madello explained the whole thing to the children. "When the annual rains fall, this bean will open up and the orange door will fall away. From the bean will come a blue moth who will live for just one day, neither eating nor sleeping. She will lay her eggs upon the leaves of the 'plant of the arrows', and when those eggs hatch into caterpillars, the tiny grubs will bore their ways into the centres of the seed pods, or beans. Soon the sun shines again and the pods burst

68

open, showering on to the ground. And, children, you must remember that the caterpillar is still inside the bean."

"So the caterpillar makes the bean jump?" asked Pablo.

"The tiny caterpillar has been busy lining the seed pod with silk which it makes itself," said the teacher. "Then it anchors its back legs to one side of the bean and is able to make the bean move by using a series of telescoping jumps. If the bean has fallen in the sunlight, the inside temperature will be too hot for the caterpillar, so it will continue to jump and jump until the temperature goes down. Notice how all these beans in the shade do not move at all, but those in the strong sunlight will continue to move until they reach the shade."

They sat there, talking about the bean moth and the wonderful *yerba de flecha* plant, and soon it was time to make their way back to the village. Señor Madello was so engrossed in the discussion as they climbed down the mountain track that it was not for quite a few minutes that he noticed Pablo was missing. Telling the children to wait for him, he returned to the shadow of Bean Rock and found Pablo standing before it, his eyes wide open in wonder.

"Señor!" he cried. "Señor Madello! The rock moved! Bean Rock moves like a Mexican jumping bean!"

Señor Madello did not know whether to laugh, or be very angry with the boy. "I have had to leave the children and come all the way back here to collect you," he said. "Really, Pablo—I thought you would have more consideration than that."

"But the Bean Rock moves!" Pablo said, ignoring his teacher's complaints.

"Rubbish!" snapped Señor Madello. "It is a rock, not a bean. How can it move??"

"It did!" said Pablo. "I saw it!"

69

"Enough," Señor Madello said. "Hurry up, Pablo. We must rejoin the children as quickly as possible."

By the time they got back to the children, Señor Madello was in a better mood, and he laughed and told the children what Pablo had said. "Young Pablo González has played a trick on me," he explained. "He made me climb the mountain again and told me that Bean Rock was moving like the jumping beans we were talking about."

"Ooh, Pablo," scolded Conchita. "That was naughty of you!"

Pablo followed on behind the group, looking back up the mountain path so that he could, whenever they turned a corner, catch a glimpse of Bean Rock. He was positive that the rock had moved.

"Perhaps we should all return to Bean Rock in the rainy season," Señor Madello said suddenly. "We may be lucky enough to see the grey moth emerge from the bean."

So it was agreed that Señor Madello would take them up into the mountains in a few months' time, when the rains came, and the children were very excited about it indeed.

Although Señor Madello had not made too much of Pablo's insistence about Bean Rock, the boy felt that perhaps he had been mistaken. After all, it had only moved once, reverting to its original position so that it did not look as if it had moved at all. Yet Pablo was sure that the rock *had* moved, and he was determined to go back at the weekend and watch it intently, just to make sure.

By the time the weekend came, Pablo would have forgotten all about the incident had Conchita not run across the compound of the village and asked him to take her up to collect beans. "I want to keep some here," she explained. "Then, when it rains, I will put by beans

70

outside the hut, and we can watch for the grey moth without having to run all the way up the mountain. Besides, it could rain on a day that Señor Madello does not come to teach us, then what would we do?"

Pablo had agreed to go with her. The idea was a sensible one, and he felt slightly chagrined that he had not thought of it first. When he thought about it, Pablo remembered his experience with Bean Rock and decided that he would take little Conchita with him, if only to make quite sure that the rock had not moved. The children were provided with a lunch which consisted of meat, well spiced with peppers, wrapped in a thin pancake. "If you place it on a hot rock, it will taste delicious," Pablo's mother told him.

So they set out in the morning, determined to bring back lots of jumping beans, and to enjoy the sunshine and freedom of the day. It took almost two hours for them to reach the Bean Rock, because Conchita insisted on stopping every few minutes to chase a rabbit, or sort through the coloured pebbles at the base of the mountain. Pablo did not mind in the least. He had been bored until Conchita had suggested the walk, and he was content to take his time.

"Come on," said Conchita. "It's around the next corner."

"No—it should be here," said Pablo.

"Course it isn't," Conchita shouted. "If it *was* here, it would *be* here, wouldn't it?"

They ran up the stony path for a few minutes, but Bean Rock was nowhere to be seen.

"It's gone!" said Pablo. "I knew it! I knew it had moved."

He felt Conchita's tiny hand slip into his and she stared up at him in wonderment. "Oh, Pablo!" she cried. "Do you really think it has moved?"

71

"Yes, it has," said Pablo. "Let's search for it."

But no matter where they looked, the massive Bean Rock was not to be found. Conchita, bored by the fruitlessness of the search, sat on a rock and ate her pancake, watching Pablo as he ran this way and that in search of the missing rock. "Maybe the American scientists came and took it away," she said casually.

"Of course!" Pablo smiled. "That is exactly what must have happened." He was relieved to have discovered a plausible explanation for the mystery.

The relief, however, did not entirely banish the thought of the mysterious rock from his mind during the following weeks. Whenever he saw Conchita examining her collection of beans, which she kept beneath a cool rock in the far corner of the hut where the sun would never reach them, he sensed an uneasiness inside himself. He was certain that Bean Rock had moved.

One night, days after the incident, Pablo lay awake on his straw bed, gazing up at the roof of the hut, listening to the sounds in the darkness and the steady breathing of his mother and father. And as he drifted down into the comfortable arms of sleep, he was suddenly jolted upright by an enormous explosion. The noise sent an electric thrill through his body so that he sat there, staring at the moonlight slanting in through the hut entrance, confused and frightened.

Before he had time to collect his senses, another explosion, much louder this time, shook through the hut, waking Pablo's parents. Soon there were voices coming from the other huts, startled voices, fearful voices. Pablo heard Conchita sobbing in bewilderment, and a man's gruff voice in the distance.

The next explosion was so massive that Pablo was out of the hut before he knew how he had managed to get there. He found himself standing in the compound, watching people running about, listening to the cries of terror. His father was standing next to him, a comforting hand upon his shoulder.

"What is it?" someone cried.

"A bomb!" another voice screamed. "It must be a bomb!"

"Look there it is!"

Every eye followed the trembling finger of the old man who was pointing to the far end of the compound.

It stood there, gigantic and towering over the huts, silvered by the light of the moon.

"Bean Rock!" Pablo cried. "It's Bean Rock!"

The immense rock balanced for a few seconds, then tilted forward, taking what seemed like an eternity to tumble over. The massive rock made thunderous explosions as it rolled over at the huts.

"Watch out!" cried Pablo's father. "It's coming for the huts!"

Conchita was crying now, her hands over her ears to block out the roaring of the grinding, rolling rock, her eyes wide open in horror as she watched it head straight towards the hut she had been sleeping in a few minutes ago. "No!" she screamed, breaking free from her mother's arms. "Maria is in there!"

She ran across the compound and into the hut before anyone could stop her. Alarmed, Pablo found himself running after her. He knew that she was trying to rescue her favourite doll.

"It isn't worth it!" he shouted. "Come back, Conchita!"

But he was too late. Conchita emerged from the hut, clutching the rag doll, and stood in the entrance, wondering which way to run, as Bean Rock descended on the hut like a vast mountain. Pablo grabbed her by the wrist and pulled hard, almost lifting Conchita from her feet as she followed him. Bean Rock fell on the hut, squashing it so flat that it was difficult to believe that a hut had ever been there.

73

Then it was still.

The villagers gathered cautiously around the rock. When it started to move again, everyone drew back in alarm.

"Water!" Pablo shouted. "Throw cold water over it! That isn't a rock at all. It's a gigantic bean!"

His words, no matter how ridiculous they sounded, spurred the villagers into action. Instantly someone came out of the darkness with a wooden pail and threw the contents over Bean Rock. Soon there were more buckets and more precious water being thrown at the immobile Bean Rock.

"More water!" Pablo cried. "If the bean is kept cool it will stop moving!"

He was right. After almost a half an hour of continuous showerings of water, the bean rock kept perfectly still.

"You must share our hut," Pablo's father told Conchita's now homeless parents. "In the morning we will make you another home."

When morning came, everyone was out in the compound, standing around Bean Rock. As the sun rose up over the distant mountain, the trail of devastation which Bean Rock had made on its journey down the mountain to the village could plainly be seen.

Pablo explained his theory to his father. "I think that this is a gigantic bean," he said, noticing with satisfaction that even the wise old men of the village were not disagreeing with him. "When the bean gets hot, it will try to move to a cool spot. It must have been out in the desert all yesterday."

"But what can we do about it?" Conchita's mother sobbed. "We have lost our home, and when the sun comes up, the Bean Rock will move again! It will destroy us all!"

"There is nothing we can do," Pablo's father told

them all. "We must wait and watch and pray that God will be kind to us."

"But there *is* something we can do!" Pablo said. "We can build a shelter for it. If we can keep Bean Rock still, then it will do no more damage."

"A shelter?" said Pablo's mother. "What sort of shelter?"

"Anything to keep the heat of the sun from it," Pablo explained. "If we keep the walls of the bean cool, the bean moth inside will think that it has found a shady spot, then it will sleep."

"You think there is a moth in there?" asked Conchita.

"Well, it is a caterpillar now," said Pablo. "But if we keep the rock cool, then the caterpillar will become a bean moth."

"Then let us kill it!" someone shouted. "We can hack through the orange door and kill the creature before it does any more damage!"

"If you try that," said Pablo's father in a low, serious voice, "the creature may create even more havoc in its attempts to escape. Besides, that orange door looks as hard as iron to me."

So the villagers set about the task of erecting a shelter, using some of the scattered timber from the crushed hut and making a framework. The women mixed the water with mud, treading it down firmly so that it oozed between their toes and became as clay.

By mid-morning the shelter was finished. It was built in the shape of a crescent so that the shifting sun could not shine upon the rock at any time of the day. And it worked!

"That was extremely clever of you to think of it," said Pablo's mother approvingly. His father said nothing, but Pablo could see that he was very proud.

Over the next few days, everyone helped Conchita's parents to build a new home. Even the children worked

75

hard, treading in the clay mud, working it and slapping it against the wooden framework so that the sun dried it hard like concrete. When that was done, life returned to normal in the village. The shelter over Bean Rock protected it from the heat of the sun and it remained in the same position for many, many weeks.

One day, some months after the rock had crashed down into the village, Pablo was sitting in the compound making dust pictures on the ground, when something fell from the sky and hit him on the nose. He touched it with his fingers, then examined it closely. Rain!

Although people in the village were used to hearing the children shouting and playing, that one word was enough to startle them into action. "Rain! The rains are coming!" Now there were pails and buckets placed out in the compound, and the water storage tank was uncovered so that it would fill to the brim, for when it rains in this region of Mexico it is like a flood. Men stripped off their shirts so that they could bathe in it and looked up at the black clouds as they raced across the face of the sun. "Rain!" they laughed. "It comes!"

The first few drops fell into the dust, spurting it up, disappearing almost instantly. Then more rain fell, covering the ground so fast that it could not be absorbed. Suddenly the air was filled with the noise of it!

How the villagers laughed. It was like a party, everyone standing out in the blessed shower, not caring if it drenched them to the skin. White teeth grinning from the suntanned faces, eyes upturned, hands held out so that they could feel it and luxuriate in its coldness.

Lightening snaked across the darkening sky, forking at the mountains, sizzling into the wet ground. Even the sparse weeds appeared to lift themselves up to receive the crystal rain as it torrented down upon them.

"It is good!" cried Pablo's father as he rubbed the water into his hairy chest. "The rain is good, eh?"

76

"Yes," laughed Pablo. "It is wonderful!" Someone was standing behind him and, as he turned to see who it was, a cascade of cold water enveloped him. "Aah! Mother!" he laughed.

"It is time you had a bath!" his mother cried, as she emptied the rest of the water from the bucket over him. Other villagers who had been watching and laughing now joined in the fun. They knew that the rains would last for some time and, for an hour or so at least, there would be the luxury of water to waste. Soon they were all throwing buckets of water at each other, much as children throw balls of snow in colder countries.

Later when they were exhausted with the fun, they stood or sat around, allowing the rains to wash over them and cleanse their bodies. It was a happy time.

Suddenly there was a loud rumbling noise, quite unlike the thunder which they had heard in the distance. All eyes turned fearfully to the shelter behind which Bean Rock lay.

"The rainy season!" Pablo cried. "Now the bean moth will appear!"

Before he could utter another word, Bean Rock crashed through the mud wall and rolled into the centre of the compound, almost knocking an old man over. Now the orange door lay uppermost, and they could all see it moving.

"It's coming out!" a young man screamed. "Quickly! Arm yourselves! The giant bean moth is coming!"

Panic spread among the people as they scurried this way and that way, searching for sticks, or spades, or forks. "Kill it!" they shrieked. "Kill the monster!"

The orange door exploded from the bean, causing everyone to freeze like statues, then a thin, wavering feeler extended from the darkness, followed by another. "It's coming!" the people cried.

Now the rain had stopped, and the sun was piercing

down, drying up the puddles so that the air was filled with steam. They watched as the enormous bean moth struggled out of the shell and fell to the ground exhausted. Sánchez, the strongest young man in the village, ran over to it with a garden fork and stood by the head, the fork raised up ready to thrust down.

"No!" Pablo cried. "Leave it alone, Sánchez! The bean moth is helpless. Can't you see that?"

"Soon it will be strong!" Sánchez replied. "When the sun has dried its wings it will be strong, and we will not be able to fight it."

"But it lives only for a single day!" Pablo implored. "Please, Sánchez. Don't harm it!"

Pablo's father joined in. "Perhaps it would be better to leave it," he said. "It would be a pity to kill it."

There was no work done that day. All the members of the village sat around the exhausted bean moth and watched it gather strength.

"When it is ready to fly, we must keep well away," said Pablo's father. "Those wings are large enough to break a man's leg without effort."

As the sun was sinking behind the blue-tinged mountains, the bean moth stirred.

"Keep back!" Sánchez cried. "If it comes towards us, I will have to kill it!"

Pablo watched as the gigantic creature spread its vast leathery wings and tested them in the air. The wings moved like two collosal blue sails, causing the air to be whipped into a wind so that it blew into the faces and the hair of the villagers. Now that the moth was strong it tried to fly, but the first effort was unsuccessful. Again it tried, writhing and stumbling as its new-found wings beat at the air, making roaring, whistling noises which filled Pablo's ears.

Then it flew!

Like an oversized aircraft the bean moth swung up

The gigantic creature spread its vast leathery wings . . .

from the ground into the air, the noise from the wings deafening everyone.

"It flies!" Sánchez yelled, his mouth splitting into a wide, white grin. "See how it flies!"

Twice the stupendous monster circled the village, its thick wings blotting out the sun as it passed before it. Then it veered away and made for the mountains, flying at great speed until it became a speck in the sky.

That evening, when they were all gathered around the roaring fire in the compound, the villagers congratulated Pablo. "How would *we* have known to keep the bean cool so that it would not move?" asked one.

They all agreed that Pablo had saved the village from almost certain destruction.

"And now we have an added advantage!" Pablo's mother said in her quiet voice. "The bean shell is large enough to act as a cistern for us to store water in!"

But that was not the end of the story of Bean Rock.

When Pablo had told the villagers all he knew about the bean moth and its habits, his father said: "I am sure that there are many children in foreign countries who know nothing at all about the bean moth. Perhaps we could take just a few beans and sell them to the schools?"

And that is precisely what they did!

Now, in place of the fifteen mud huts, there are over twenty nice new houses in the village. Pablo's father has a new leather shop, and most of the villagers are employed collecting the *yerba* beans and placing them in plastic tubes to be sent all over the world to educate children in the ways of nature.

If ever you should happen to go to the village in the future, a bright-eyed young man named Pablo will be delighted to tell you the story of the Bean Rock Monster, just as he told it to me. But, for those of you unable to make the visit, I asked his permission to tell you all about it.

MONSTER IN DISTRESS

By Patricia Moynehan

Sybilla Cowan was twelve when her family moved to North Yorkshire. Her father had acquired the position of curator of the local museum and, with it, the tenancy of a large house situated on the edge of bleak, open moors. A rather grim structure built of grey stone, their new home was two storeys high and heavily roofed with flags, in order to resist the winds that might have stripped off a lighter covering.

But one small area of the vast, undulating moor was protected by woodland; an island of stunted firs, all stretching their gaunt limbs in one direction, as though begging alms from the sun. Sybilla, a child who liked her own company, often wandered into this shadow-haunted labyrinth, which—so she imagined—was saturated with the lingering aroma of a long—dead age. But it was not long before she realised that there was a strange absence of small life in this isolated place; no reassuring sound of bird song, or the stealthy rustle of undergrowth that would have announced the presence of a leveret, going about his lawful business. Only the eerie sigh of the never-resting wind, that sometimes rose to the likeness of a despairing shriek.

But Sybilla was drawn to the place, aware of a burning need to venture deep into the winding glades, that were carpeted by an obscene, grey moss, which bore a disturbing resemblance to hair on an old man's head.

Then suddenly, weeks after moving into Moor House, she found the ruined castle.

Like a besieging army, the stunted trees encircled the

fortress's shattered walls, although they did not encroach on a wide strip of black earth that may have been a filled-in moat.

Sybilla clambered over a pile of crumbling masonry and stepped on to the former inner ward, then looked up at the donjon (later she had cause to wonder how she knew its correct name), that was still in a reasonable state of preservation. The roof had gone, and the four turrets looked like grey, jagged teeth, but the doorway was intact, and the long, narrow loopholes retained their original shape.

Sybilla walked through the doorway and cautiously wended her way across the stone-littered floor, which was now highlighted by the sun that streamed down from the open roof. She decided the castle must have been quite a small one, possibily a fort built in the troubled Dark Ages, then deserted when more peaceful times returned. At regular intervals, jutting stones marked the position of upper floors, while, to the left of the doorway, three stone steps were all that remained of a once spiral stairway.

"The grave of a dead age," Sybilla whispered, and the softly uttered words were seized by a sudden gust of wind that came blustering over the floor, raising swirling eddies of dust that seemed to converge on the young intruder. Then the wind died as abruptly as it had come into being, and a dreadful silence descended upon the ruined castle. When Sybilla walked towards the east wall, her footsteps sent out disturbing echoes that created the impression of an invisible being following her, making her look fearfully back over one shoulder.

Then the unexpected happened. The floor gave way beneath her feet and, with a gasping cry, the young girl went down into a gaping hole, to land with a body-shaking thud on to a fortunately dust-cushioned floor below. For a while, Sybilla dared not move, certain she must have at least broken a leg, but presently her breath returned and, with it, reassurance that she had suffered no injury. Looking up, she realised she was now about three metres below ground level and had fallen into a subterranean room that might once have been a storage place, or even a dungeon. It would now be necessary to build some kind of platform if she was to climb back to safety.

But this proved to be no easy task, for most of the fallen masonry that littered the floor was either too small, or too heavy, for a not over-strong girl to carry. She was beginning to experience the first pangs of panic when her eye detected the sagging wall that loomed just beyond the circle of light cast by the sun, that sent its golden rays down through the ruined battlements.

A number of stone slabs, measuring some fifteen by twenty centimetres, had already fallen down, and it would be an easy matter to dislodge some more from the tottering wall. Much encouraged by this prospect, Sybilla began to build her platform, piling layer upon layer of slabs on top of one another, making certain that each succeeding level was a little narrower than the last, thus forming a most satisfactory flight of steps.

But she had soon used up all of the fallen stones and was forced to turn her attention to the wall, which she attacked with more energy than foresight, with the result that the entire structure came tumbling down with a resounding crash, to say nothing of a choking cloud of dust. Sybilla, who had jumped back just in time, spent a good five minutes coughing and congratulating herself on providing an unlimited supply of platform-building material, before taking note of the large aperture that was now revealed.

Fortunately a little more of the ceiling had come down, thus permitting the sunlight to illuminate the room that was now completely visible beyond a pile of rubble and stone slabs.

Sybilla rubbed her eyes, blinked, then pinched herself to make certain she was not dreaming. But without any possible doubt, there was a large, rectangular block of stone standing in the very centre of the room, and on it a small wooden chest. The word "treasure" went streaking across her brain like a flash of lightning on a dark night. It took but a short time for her to scramble over the rubble and enter the recently exposed chamber, while keeping a wary eye on what remained of the ceiling.

Possibly "chest" was too grand a word, for the box was not more than thirty centimetres long, by twenty wide and fifteen deep. Sybilla wiped the dust away with her handkerchief, then emitted an involuntary cry of pleasure when she saw the blue opal set into the centre of the lid. It glittered in the sunlight, took on iridescent reflections when she moved the box from side to side, and once even captured the image of her own face, which stared up at her with microscopic eyes.

Sybilla carried the casket (a more satisfactory definition) back over the fallen wall and, after placing it on the floor, set about completing her platform. Presently she clambered up into the main keep, clutching the box under one arm, barely controlling an urge to open it and find out what was inside. But a detailed examination failed to discover a lock or hinges, just an almost imperceptible thin line that marked the position of a lid.

Sybilla said: "Botheration!"—her favourite expression whenever she was annoyed, then decided to go straight home and let her father solve the mystery. After all, he was curator of a museum, and opening old boxes should be an easy matter for him.

She had left the donjon and was scrambling over the outer wall, when a disturbing sound made her stop and look fearfully back over one shoulder. It began as a roar, then rose up to a long-drawn-out shriek, and seemed to come from beneath the castle. It lasted for possibly twenty seconds, but to Sybilla it seemed like twenty years, particularly when the box—again tucked under her left arm—quivered slightly, as though something inside was trying to get out.

The sound died away, merged into the murmuring wind as a despairing sigh, and Sybilla broke into a run, raced through the dim glades of the shadow-haunted wood at a speed she normally would have considered an impossibility. She came out on to the open moorland and there paused for a while to regain her breath. Rather reluctantly, she took the casket in both hands and shook it gently. There was no sound of rattling, or thudding, which might have suggested it contained a hard or soft object. After a while, Sybilla decided that fear is food for the imagination, and the cry she had heard was nothing more than an owl who had been awakened by her intrusion, and it was she who had been quivering, not the casket. Comforted by this satisfactory explanation, she walked slowly home.

Mr Cowan was eating his lunch and, as Sybilla was late, he declined to examine the wooden box, no matter how old it might be. But when he had drunk his second cup of coffee, his curiosity would not be denied, and, after pushing a plate to one side, he placed the box on the table and surveyed it with lively interest.

"Made of oak, I'd say. Old—very old. Doesn't seem to have any hinges or a lock. Where did you find it?"

"In a dungeon in an old castle I found in the woods."

Mr Cowan frowned. "You mean that place they call Dead Man's Wood?"

"I didn't know it was called that."

"I don't like you going to that place. It's got some kind of bad reputation. Anyway, I don't think this box is worth much. But clean it up and maybe I'll have another look at it this evening."

In fact, removing the grime accumulated over many centuries proved to be an impossible task, and although Sybilla scrubbed the wood with warm water and fine sand, she was never able to do more than give the box a kind of clean, dirty appearance. Neither, despite much pulling and jerking, could she raise the lid, a fact that afforded her a strange sense of relief. But the blue opal, which was about eight centimetres in diameter, glittered like a solitary star in a black sky, looking at times extremely beautiful, at others rather sinister.

Finally, Sybilla took the casket up to her bedroom, where she placed it on the windowsill, the only available space that would do it justice. When her father came home he was in no mood to discuss the old wooden box, being gravely concerned about an act of vandalism at the museum, which had resulted in considerable damage to a number of exhibits. Having exhausted the subject during dinner, he shut himself in his study, leaving Sybilla and her mother to occupy themselves as they wished.

The television presented a parade of mundane programmes that sent Mrs Cowan to sleep and did not allow Sybilla to concentrate on her holiday task, that regretfully was scarcely begun. Then, when the mantelpiece clock struck ten, Mr Cowan came out of his study and, after yawning, said: "Time for Bedfordshire," and started to turn out lights. Sybilla gave her parents a dutiful kiss and went upstairs to her own room.

Before getting into bed, she looked out of the window and stood for a while, admiring the rolling moors which had been turned into a silver wonderland by the full moon. Suddenly a cloud shadow came racing across the purple heather, creating the impression that an unformed ghost was fleeing before an invisible pursuer. It glided over the hedge, across the unkempt lawn, then disappeared in the block of black shadow cast by the house. From far away, possibly in the vicinity of Dead Man's Wood, a mournful cry rose up to the twinkling stars. Sybilla shuddered and literally ran to her bed, where she nestled down under the sheets and blankets, hoping that whatever could not be seen, did not exist. Sleep crept upon her unawares; it seemed as if at one moment she was telling herself that this was going to be a long, worrying, wide-awake night; the next she was being rocketed up from a deep pit of oblivion, crying out: "What was that?"

The room was awash with moonlight, which appeared to make every item of furniture rear up from a nest of darkness. Sybilla looked frantically from wardrobe to dressing-table, then to the nasty dark corner on the left of the door, knowing that some unexpected sound had awakened her. At length—like a bird being drawn to a hissing snake—her head slowly turned, and she saw the wooden casket standing on the windowsill.

The lid lay a few centimetres to the right, and the blue opal was sending out a pulsating light, which, in itself, was a most alarming phenomenon. But Sybilla could only stare at the open box. Four white fingers were crawling over the front, struggling to get a firm grip, while a slender thumb waved back and forth in the moonlight. Suddenly, after a horrible jerking movement, the hand jumped out of the box, to land with a soft thud on the shelf, there to lay motionless for a few moments, as though gathering strength for its next move.

It ran, using all four fingers as legs, to the nearest curtain, which it gripped between forefinger and thumb, then slid gracefully down to the floor. Sybilla watched it scurry across the carpet in the direction of her writing desk, before again taking refuge under the bedclothes. Presently her terror was increased by hearing a faint scratching sound, such as might be made by a sharp object being applied to a smooth surface. Greatly daring, Sybilla pushed her head out into the open and gasped when she saw the hand on her desk, a pencil gripped between index finger and thumb, writing something on a sheet of paper. Then it dropped the pencil, did a little dance on the tips of its fingers, before jumping on to a chair, climbing down on one leg and racing back across the floor.

Once again, Sybilla went down under the bedclothes and remained there for a full five minutes, until it was reasonable to suppose that the hand had gone back into the box. When she again forced herself to look across the room, there was no sign of a detached hand, and the blue opal had ceased to send out a flickering light. It took great courage to climb out of bed and approach the window, even more to peer into the open box and take note of the beautiful white hand that lay with the thumb and little finger outstretched, so that the dreadful thing was wedged firmly. Sybilla took a deep breath, then took up the lid, which she slammed over the casket with a resounding snap.

Curiosity made her walk to the desk and, after turning on a lamp, read what was written in a neat, rounded hand on the sheet of paper. The phraseoloy was old-fashioned, the spelling dreadful, but the meaning perfectly clear.

Knoo ye that I, Charles Carstairs, third Earl of Manley, beeing of grate conceit, did in ye twenty-first year of mye life and ye thirty-fifth of ye rein of ye glorious Elizabeth, gaze upon mye reflection and greeve that time wood erase mye bewty, witch was indede wunderous to beholde. Then did I, bye divers meens, seek out Manfred the Black, who men saye has prolonged his earthly existence bye meny lifetimes, and offered him muche gold for ye gift of nether dimmed youth.

He spake to me thus: "Not all ye gold of Eldorado canst purchase that witch ye seek, for unending youth is beyond price. But it can bee yores for a small gift. Yore right hand. Indeed will that bee a grivious loss, but better lose won hand, than ye intire body, witch will bee consumed bye time."

Verily shood I have knoun him for ye evil creeture that hee was, butt mye conceit wood brook noe denial and I must doo what hee ask. I drank ye contocshon hee prepaired and knew noo moor untill I wache in this place. O, most merciful God, lete the memory bee blotted out. I was in a seecret place under ye cascel and, throo a grid set in ye dore, saw a mann with a compleet likeness to mye self, butt who had a claw for a right hand. Hee held a boxe in witch laye mye right hand that did writhe wen I cryed out in a harsh voice.

Mye image spake: "Knoo ye not that ye right hand is an extensoon of ye sole? We have nowe exchanged bodys, but myne hast now ye shape in witch I was creeated. Ye are indeedd hideous too beholde. Eturnal youth ist yores and heer in this place will ye live forever til the son grows cold. Butt it bee decreed ye have a spark of hope. Wen innosense overcomes feer and dares to return yore right hand—alone and unaided—then shall ye be free."

Hee left mee thus, and wen cascel was destroyed, I beeleve hee perished, butt I live on in this oresum shape. Have mercie on him who was once Charles Carstairs, third Earl of Manley.

Sybilla folded the sheet of paper and placed it in her desk drawer, then went back to bed, where she gave the matter her full consideration. If the monster, which had once been the young earl, was under the castle, he must be in some subterranean room that lay beyond or beneath the one she had fallen into. Would she have the courage to clamber among those dangerous ruins in an effort to find it? Then there was the prospect of facing a dreadful-looking creature and returning its right hand.

Of course, she could always tell her father what had happened, show him the paper, and, if he wanted any further proof, make him smash the box and see the hand for himself. But the instruction was most explicit: innocence (herself) had to return the hand alone and unaided. Then she remembered the mournful cry and came to an irrevocable decision.

"I'll do it," she said aloud. "But first I must find out more about the young earl."

The assistant librarian was most helpful and found a massive volumn in the reference library that contained a full history of the surrounding district. Sybilla turned eagerly to the period which covered the reign of Elizabeth the First and presently settled down to read a chapter headed:

CHARLES CARSTAIRS, THIRD EARL OF MANLEY

Charles, born in 1564, was, from all contemporary accounts, a sweet, amiable youth until a little after his twenty-first birthday. Possessed of exceptional physical beauty (of which he was inordinately proud), he was admired by all who knew him and worshipped by all the ladies of the neighbouring families. But some time during the year 1585 he would appear to have suffered a terrible injury that affected both mind and body. From that time, his right hand was covered by a black velvet glove, and from being a kindly, well-intentioned, if somewhat weak youth, he was transformed into a vicious, evil man who was soon hated and feared by the entire countryside. It was said he kept a terrible monster deep under the castle, reputed to be none other than Manfred the Black, a legendary sorcerer who had bewitched him.

Whatever the reason for this inexplicable change, the local people rose up against the earl in 1590, when he was put to death and the castle destroyed. One account states that his right hand had been replaced by a hideous claw.

See page 245 for a sixteenth century plan of Manley Castle.

90

Sybilla quickly turned to page 245 and was delighted to find a scale drawing of the castle, followed by a detailed explanation.

Manley Castle was built in 1136, intended, no doubt, to serve as an outpost for King Stephen's forces during the civil war which raged between him and the Empress Matilda. It is of special interest in so far as the donjon is equipped with a double-tier dungeon system, the top layer serving as storage rooms, while the lower housed prisoners and those who guarded them.

As will be seen from the contemporary plan, the upper storey was connected to the lower by means of a spiral stairway, situated in the left, furthermost corner of the donjon. When the castle was under attack, this was sealed by a massive stone slab.

Sybilla had read enough and concentrated her attention on the drawing, which most certainly depicted the double row of dungeons and a spiral stairway that, so far as she could judge, was about six metres from the place where she found the casket. Now the dividing wall had collapsed she should have no difficulty in finding it, but raising a heavy stone and going down into a dark, dismal place and facing whatever lurked below was another matter.

The following afternoon, Mr and Mrs Cowan departed for the Yorkshire Antiquarian Society Conference which was being held in a nearby town, and their absence enabled Sybilla to embark on her hair-raising adventure. She first found a stout bag, and into this she placed a large hammer, a cold chisel, an electric torch and the wooden casket. Thus equipped, she set out to restore a right hand to a despairing monster.

She crossed the moor in bright sunshine, then, after saying a little prayer, entered Dead Man's Wood. Here, only a few shafts of light were permitted to invade the gloom, and the guarded trees stretched out gaunt arms, as though trying to clutch the intruder. But when Sybilla reached the castle, the jagged walls were positively gleaming, while cringing shadows huddled in obscure corners, like frightened animals sheltering from a storm.

It was an easy matter for her to descend into what she now knew to be the first layer of underground rooms, for the rough platform was till standing, but it was a little more difficult to clamber over the rumble and into the space where the casket had been found. Here Sybilla switched on the torch and sent its powerful beam across the room highlighting a carpet of dust, fallen masonry, pieces of rotting wood that might once have been crates —and an arched doorway that looked as if it led to somewhere very nasty.

Carrying her bag in one hand and the torch in the other, she entered a room where three walls were covered with stone shelves, while the fourth was broken by another doorway that led out on to a small landing. Here a short flight of steps ran down to an enclosed space that appeared to be without any purpose, for it was too small to store anything, being not more than two metres square, and certainly had no visible outlet. Sybilla directed her torch beam downwards, then scraped some of the dust to one side with the heel of her shoe. A thin line was revealed.

She was standing on the stone slab which covered the spiral staircase leading down to the lower dungeons.

To find was one matter—to open quite another. Sybilla hammered the hard stone until her arm ached; tried to drive the cold chisel into the surrounding crack, and only succeeded in blunting its sharp edge. Having acquired a painful blister on one hand, she leaned against one wall and fought back tears of frustration.

It was indeed a strange position to be in. Sybilla was

92

very disappointed in not being able to raise the stone slab, but, at the same time, did not at all relish facing whatever waited for her below. Finally, overcome by this conflict of emotions, she banged her clenched fist on the wall and cried out: "Oh, why did I have to come here in the first place?"

The answer was a low rumbling sound, and the stone slab slowly tilted until it appeared to stand on edge, one half in a gaping hole, the other rearing up above the floor. By banging the wall, Sybilla had solved her problem, for clearly a loose brick was in some way connected with a mechanism that opened a medieval trap door. When she shone her torch into the opening, there was a curving, stone stairway, leading down to the nether regions, from which came an unpleasant smell that was a mixture of stale air and damp earth.

With a deep sigh, Sybilla took up her bag and began to descend the steps. The walls curved round and round, and several times she had to stop and carve her way through a mass of dense cobwebs, but at last she came down into a long passage that was lined on either side by a row of rusty iron doors. Sybilla stopped and, after directing her torch beam first to the left, then to the right, called out in a tremulous voice: "Ex . . . excuse me . . . but is there anyone here?"

Her question went echoing along the passage, and it seemed as if another voice sent back the last words: "Anyone . . . one . . . one . . . here . . . here . . . here?" Then that awful cry came into being—a low moan that quickly grew into a bellowing roar, that in turn became a wailing shriek. Sybilla's first inclination was to bolt up the steps and not stop running until she was back on the open moors, but when the cry ceased and was succeeded by a series of harsh sobs, pity overcame fear, and she was just able to creep along the passage, drawing floor, gradually nearer to the distressing sound.

The passage was terminated by a very large door that had an iron grid in the centre, and it was from behind this that the violent sobbing came. Sybilla knew with an awful certainty that her search was over; now she must look upon the unthinkable.

Two iron bars, resting in sockets set in the wall on either side of the door, had to be removed; then a great black handle had to be turned, before Sybilla could pull and hear the protesting groans of rusty hinges, as the heavy portal swung slowly open. Then she again took up her torch and, after a long pause, swung the beam of light into the cell.

It was standing up. About two metres tall, with an immense round head in which deep-set red eyes were the most outstanding features, the creature had two tiny horns, which grew out of a mass of coarse red hair and were a perfect match for the curving fangs that deformed the jutting chin. Deep lines formed an intricate pattern over the yellow face, creating the impression that it was covered with old, rotting parchment. Rolls of fat encased the neck, which was in complete contrast to the near-skeletal body, where skin-covered bones could be seen between patches of black fur. A bulging stomach surmounted a pair of bowed and extremely thin legs, while grotesquely long arms dangled down to knee level, one terminating in a curved claw, the other in a red, raw stump.

The monster shuffled forward a little way, then made a low growling sound that gradually assumed a crude semblance to speech.

"Caasket . . . down . . . on . . . floor . . ."

Sybilla swallowed and managed to speak "You . . . you want me to put the casket on the floor?"

The monster inclined its head and emitted a growl that could have been interpreted as a prolonged "yes". Sybilla advanced into the cell, placed the casket on the

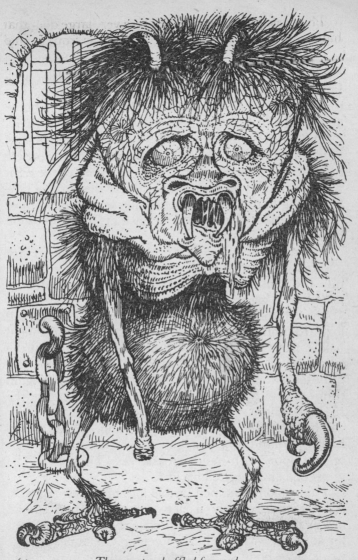

The monster shuffled forward . . .

floor, then quickly retreated when the blue opal began to send out a pulsating light. As she watched with gaping mouth and wonder-filled eyes, the lid flew off and went clattering across the floor, coming to rest by the far wall. Four fingers slid over the box front, a thumb wriggled up to join them, then the entire hand dropped to the floor and went scuttling over to the now motionless monster.

The hand hopped on to a taloned foot, began a slow journey up the left leg, over the bulging stomach, there to be seized by a gigantic claw. The stump of the right wrist moved to the left and was there met by the now trembling hand; both came together with a soft, almost imperceptible thud—and an instant transformation began to take place.

The monster gave a last prolonged shriek as its face and body appeared to melt; the hair quivered and sank into the skull, which, in turn, seethed as though subjected to a great heat. Nose, mouth and eyes all disappeared under a cloud of steam, and the creature fell forward and writhed on the floor. Sybilla screamed before running from the cell and taking refuge at the very end of the passage. After the lapse of some five minutes, she found the courage to go back, walking on tiptoe, prepared to retreat again should there be the slightest sound.

The cloud of steam was dispersing, revealing the body of a handsome young man, who lay stretched out on the floor, both hands crossed over his breast. The ghost of a smile parted his lips.

This vision remained visible for only a few seconds. Almost immediately a network of wrinkles spread across the face, as though time, angry at being cheated for so long, was in a hurry to complete its destructive work. The body shrank, became nothing more that a skin-covered skeleton, an ugly mockery of the beauty the earl wished to retain forever.

Sybilla picked up the casket, recovered the lid and fitted the one on to the other. The blue opal was now a dull, not very interesting stone, and the lid could be taken off and replaced without any difficulty at all. She left the cell, closed the door and went back down the passage. There could no possibility that she would ever visit this place again.

Maybe the Earl of Manley had found everlasting beauty at last. The beauty of eternal tranquillity.

CAPTAIN CASTLETON'S BISCUIT BEETLE

By Daphne Froome

"Biscuit beetles!" Captain Castleton shouted, banging his fist hard down on to the desk and glaring across at the children standing uncertainly behind their father. "Biscuit beetles—*giant* biscuit beetles at that! I've never, in all my days in sail, come across such creatures. I'm not like your common sailors, calling just about everything that attacks a biscuit a weevil. More often that not they mean biscuit beetles—and these *were* biscuit beetles and no doubt about it. The biscuits you supplied me with must have been alive with the things!"

"My biscuits?" Mr Nichols, the children's father, frowned. "I've not had any other complaints. I'm willing to wager there were no beetles in the biscuits when I sold them to you—you must have picked them up in Spain."

"They were specially good biscuits," David Nichols protested fiercely. He hated to see his father so upset. "And made with extra-nourishing ingredients."

Captain Castleton snorted. "They certainly nourished the beetles all right. And I have another complaint to make. We ran out of biscuits well before the end of the voyage—you must have given us short weight."

"I never give short weight." The children's father looked worried.

"Well, anyway," the captain replied firmly, "I want my money back."

Ann Nichols did quick sums in her head. Though she was younger than her brother David, she was better at

98

adding and subtracting. "But you bought ever so many biscuits. You can't have all your money back," she protested. "We'll scarce have enough to buy food if you do."

The captain laughed sarcastically. "You can live on your own beetly biscuits then. If you don't give me my money back, I'll see none of my friends buys from you either. I've plenty of time—I've docked for a fortnight."

"Run along children, at once, do you hear?" Mr Nichols' voice was sharp, so sharp that the children needed no second bidding, but dodged from behind the desk and ran through the door of the house and out on to the quay.

Glancing through the window as they passed, Ann could see that Captain Castleton was leaning forward, his face very close to her father's, the back of his smart, white-curled wig fairly vibrating with rage above the collar of his heavily brocaded coat. "How I hate that man!" she muttered, beginning to run to keep up with her brother's long strides. "Bullying father like that!"

David led the way past a crowd of sailors and round a stack of lobster pots. He began to wish that his father had not become so fascinated by this newfangled science of chemistry. No one really minded him spending all his spare time in the attic, boiling and bubbling strange liquids, but even David, who was almost as keen on chemistry as his father, had been worried when Mr Nichols had insisted on adding one of his particularly potent concoctions to the mixture used for making Captain Castleton s ship's biscuits.

"It'll nourish the crew, my boy; buck 'em up no end," his father had assured him confidently. "And with a captain like Castleton, goodness knows they need it!"

David pushed the worry from his mind and turned to his sister. "It's not easy being a ship chandler, supplying goods to all kinds of captains. Father's ways saying how lucky he is with his customers, on the whole; there's bound to be the odd one who makes a fuss. The trouble is, Captain Castleton's a very influential and rich man.'"

"Perhaps he got rich by getting his money back all the time. I wish we were just half as rich as he is." Ann paused longingly beside a stall piled high with exotic-looking tropical shells, then ran on to catch up with her brother again.

David had stopped at the edge of the jetty to study Captain Castleton's ship, trying to convince himself that she really wasn't the grandest of all the vessels moored in the little harbour. He stood in awe, gazing up at the two giant masts of the schooner, the complicated patterns of rigging, and the neatly furled sails, silhouetted against the blue sky. "Can't you imagine her, with all her sails set, racing through the water?" he asked excitedly. "I bet there's no end of a view from up on the mast top. I wish Captain Castleton would let me go on board, just once."

"You know he won't. You've asked him ever so many times," said Ann in a matter-of-fact tone.

A burly sailor shouted at them from the deck. "Out of the way now, you children—do you want to get yourselves killed? Can't you see we're just about to start unloading?"

Ann and David retreated to a safe distance and watched as the men set to work with cranes, hauling cases of oranges out of the hold and swinging them over on to the quay.

Ann studied the ship's figurehead, a rather scornful-looking woman, she thought, with long black hair flowing away from a face in which two dark eyes glared at her with a malicious glance not unlike that of Captain Castleton. "I don't like this ship at all," she grumbled. "I'm going home."

"Oh, all right, but how about coming back later, tonight perhaps? We might be able to sneak on board unnoticed then. The captain always stays at the George Inn, and most of the crew leave the ship once they've finished unloading."

"Supposing we get caught?"

"If your scared I'll come back on my own," David answered loftily.

"Of course I'm not scared," protested Ann. "I'll come with you."

The quay seemed a very different place at night, and the cobbled walk leading from their house to the place where the schooner was moored was thronged with dark shadows. Ann clung to her brother's arm, and paused, trying not to tremble, beside the gangplank that led up on to the deck.

"I told you the ship would be deserted," David whispered. "There's only the old night-watchman and he's sound asleep." He led the way up the gangplank and pointed to a figure seated on an upturned box and leaning heavily against the rail. Its cap had fallen over one eye, its mouth was wide open, and its eyes tight shut. "Some watchman!" David grinned to himself, then ran quickly round the deck, thrusting his head in at the galley. "No cooking going on," he remarked. "I knew they'd all have gone ashore." He darted across the deck and put his hands on the wheel. "I'm the helms-man," he declared. "Helm's a'lee, sir!"

"Whatever does that mean?"

"It means the helm's been put over to the lee side, stupid, and everyone has to dash around pulling on the ropes."

"If you keep on shouting like that you'll wake the watchman," Ann retorted.

"Let's go below then." David had picked up a lantern

and was already climbing down the ladder into the blackness of the hold. "My word, it's larger than I thought, like a great, empty hall now they've unloaded all the oranges." He began to walk along the thirty or so metres to the other end, the lantern flickering uncertainly as he moved, his footsteps echoing on the bare wooden boards, whistling under his breath like he always did when he was frightened and didn't want to show it. He stopped at the end, and the hold became very silent.

"Listen," he suddenly said. "What's that noise?"

"What noise? I can't hear anything."

"Of course you can't if you keep talking all the time," David answered hotly. "It seems to be coming from the other side of this partition."

Ann made her way rather uncertainly round a pile of empty sacks, ran to her brother's side, and they both stood listening. "It's a kind of champing sound," she exclaimed. "Almost like something munching."

"It must be a pretty large something, whatever it is, to make as much noise as that," David replied.

"It's coming through," she screamed.

They leaped back just as the wooden partition splintered, and a large, round, reddish-brown head, with a pair of enormous protruding eyes, thrust its way towards them. Two very long feelers came snaking outwards, followed by two front legs, two middle and two back ones, taking the creature's weight as it heaved its armoured body through the hole towards them.

"It's got wings—it's flying!" The monster became airborne, and suddenly dived towards them. Ann threw herself to the floor, her head buried in her arms.

"Quick, run!" David seized his sister's hand, dragged her to her feet and back the way they had come, not pausing until they reached the bottom of the ladder leading up on to the deck. Then he turned and peered uncertainly into the gloom. "I can't see it, or hear it either," he gasped breathlessly. "It doesn't seem to be following us. It must have gone back. Whatever can it be? Some sort of a monster beetle?"

"I think it's a biscuit beetle, like Captain Castleton was talking about," Ann answered, shakily. "I've seen a picture of one in a book. They start off as eggs, turn into grubs that eat great holes in the biscuits, and end up as beetles. Perhaps Captain Castleton was telling the truth after all! It certainly is the kind that's found in biscuits, I'm sure, and it looked as if it's covered with biscuit crumbs now."

David thought again of the way his father had weighed out on his balance strange-looking crystals that he said made people happy; the liquid he had filtered that was supposed to make people strong; the odd-looking powder he had ground up in his pestle and mortar. "All absolutely harmless," his father had said as he had added them to the biscuit mixture. "They can do nothing but good." David vowed *he* would never play around with chemicals he did not understand. He thought wryly that, if anything, Captain Castleton looked thinner and meaner than ever, while the beetle, as it ate more and more of the biscuits, had grown larger and larger. Perhaps it had grown so large because it had lived on practically nothing else.

"What a monster it is! It's bigger than we are. And goodness knows how much fuss the captain would have made if he'd seen a thing like this." David laughed uncertainly. "No wonder he thought father had given him short weight with this thing eating its way through the supplies."

"Oh, I'm sure I can hear it coming this way!" Ann raced up the ladder with David close behind her.

As they reached the top, they suddenly heard Captain Castleton's voice, rapping out orders, not shouting, as he usually did, but speaking in a quiet, edgy kind of tone. "Look lively now. At the rate you men work it'll be morning before we're unloading the goods and all the world will know."

The children crouched down. Peeping over the built-up rim round the edge of the opening, they could see that the deck was quite crowded with busy, stealthily moving figures.

"Do you think we dare make a dash for it?" Ann breathed.

David regarded the long strip of moonlit deck between them and the gangplank. "We wouldn't stand a chance—it's as bright as day. Look out, someone's spotted us!"

Ann found herself hastily pulled to the bottom of the ladder. David pushed her out of sight behind a coil of rope, and snatched her hat from her head to cover the light from the lantern as heavy footsteps approached.

"Anything wrong, Ben?" someone called.

"I thought I saw something move—there's nothing here, though. I must have been mistaken."

The footsteps retreated again. The children waited a few minutes, then edged stealthily back to the bottom of the ladder.

"Whatever they're up to they don't want anyone to know about it. If they catch us we'll be for it," whispered David.

"I'd rather face a hundred Captain Castletons than that monster. Oh, where is it, I wonder?"

David held the lantern high and, looking around, he began to advance warily along the hold. Ann followed closely at his heels, trying not to imagine that the monster might be lurking above, ready to drop down on to them at any moment, or crouching in some hiding-place it had gnawed through the planks below, waiting for them to fall on top of it.

At last they reached the hole in the end wall. It was even larger now, and, carefully avoiding the jagged wood all round the edges, David peered nervously through. "I can't see anything," he muttered. He held the lantern in the hole, then gingerly stretched out his arm so that the light illuminated the cavity beyond. "Well, just look at this!" he cried at last. "It's all right," he added. "There's quite a large room through there, and the monster's over in the far corner."

Ann gathered all her courage, grasped the lantern in a rather unsteady hand, and took David's place. She found herself looking into another compartment, obviously a secret one, divided off by this thin, wooden partition from the prying gaze of the Customs men should they come to inspect the hold. The compartment was piled high with bundles and boxes. "I can see the great gap the beetle made when it came up in the first place," she said.

"Well, you've sharper eyes than I have—I didn't notice that. I reckon it's been living below there for ages."

"I expect it came up when the sailors left the ship and everything suddenly became quiet. Perhaps it's nervous."

"Who are you trying to convince?" David laughed edgily.

Ann took another look at the monster, which was stamping belligerently about in a pile of tea spilled from a shattered tea chest, its head twisting from side to side, its feelers waving as it chewed its way purposefully through a bale of fine, shining silk.

"One thing's obvious," David maintained. "Captain Castleton is a smuggler. The goods he's going to unload are all those valuable things stowed away in there with the monster."

"If only we could think of some way of getting that

105

horrid man caught," Ann said. "That would put a stop to his bullying ways."

"We're the ones who are likely to get caught, as soon as they come down here to unload all this," David answered shortly. "We might try hiding behind that coil of rope and the sacks, I suppose, but what would happen if, when the men had emptied the hold, they battened down the hatch and left us prisoners?"

"Perhaps, when they see the monster, they'll be so busy dealing with it we can slip away."

"I shouldn't think we have much chance," her brother replied. "After all, there are ever so many men and only one beetle."

Ann felt suddenly almost sorry for the great beetle.

At that moment, the ship began to tremble and creak, and they could hear the water splashing against the sides.

"We're moving," shouted David.

"The monster's staring right at me," screamed Ann. "It's sliding towards me—I know it's going to attack us!"

David ran across to the pile of sacks and, picking up as many as he could, began ramming them into the hold. "It'll take it a while to eat its way through all those," he said at last.

They pulled the coil of rope out of sight of the people up on deck, and sat perched uncomfortably on top of it, trying to listen for any sound from the monster above the rattling, bumping and curtly rapped-out orders, as the ship got under way. Every now and then, they crept fearfully round the hold, watching for the giant beetle, but it did not reappear.

"I wish it wasn't so cold." Ann jumped up and down and tried to stop her teeth from chattering. "We must have been down here for ages."

"Less than an hour I reckon. Time always goes slowly, waiting about like this."

"I bet that monster's not waiting about—I do wish I knew what it was up to."

"I'll go and look if you like; at least it will be something to do. Anything's better than just dawdling around here, wondering what's going to happen."

"I'll come and help you, then," Ann said. "I couldn't bear to be left here alone, expecting the monster to come crashing out at me at any moment."

David began to ease the sacks from the hole one by one.

"Don't let it escape!"

"I'm not that silly," David snapped. "If I give a shout, you must ram the sacks back again as quickly as you can."

"Can you see any sign of it?"

"No—I can hear it though." David suddenly looked upwards. "It's sitting right on top of the cargo. I can't see its head at all—I believe it's chewed right through the hull to the outside. Lucky it's above the water line or we'd be swamped. Look, there's a glimpse of the sky."

They climbed warily through into the secret compartment and stood watching the giant biscuit beetle as it heaved its massive body out of sight.

The children ran forward and began to climb up the tea chests, bundles and bales of silk, to the top, looking out at the monster's heavy form skimming uncertainly over the surface of the water.

"I suppose I should say I hope that's the end of the beetle," said Ann. "But really I'm hoping it will reach the shore all right."

"And I'm hoping *we* can," her brother added. "We shall have to swim for it. Look, we seem to have sailed into the estuary. We're not so very far from the sand dunes, though it's very deep just here. It's a good thing it's a fine night and the water's so calm." He was already stripping off his shirt.

Ann began to unbuckle her shoes. "I'll race you

there," she said. "I don't fancy hanging about. All the way to the shore, I shall imagine those long legs reaching down and grabbing me."

"We've left it behind by now. We're travelling at a good rate you know," David said confidently. "Dive in quietly," he added. "Then neither the monster nor the captain will hear."

They reached the shore in plenty of time to warn the Customs men of Captain Castleton's approach. The captain never did find out who had given away the secret of his smuggling activities, or what it was that had bored so many holes in his schooner.

He found languishing in a dark and dirty prison, while awaiting trial, not at all to his liking. Eventually, when the judge at the assizes set him free on payment of a fine, he was so relieved he became quite a reformed character, and the first thing he did was to give Ann and David's father back the biscuit money.

One day, some time later, after the captain had returned to sea, the children went back and explored the beaches that lay nearest to the point where the creature had flown away from the ship. They spent a long time running along the edge of the water, looking under rocks and in pools, but the giant biscuit beetle was nowhere to be seen. They ate the gingerbread their mother had given them, and were just preparing to go home when David spotted a movement in a cave half hidden behind a boulder at the top of the little bay. They ran towards it and, tentatively edging their way inside, they found the giant monster.

It paused a moment in its task of consuming a long, trailing frond of seaweed to eye them with a distinctly friendly glance. Then it swallowed the seaweed and began to attack a piece of driftwood. And, for all I know, it lives in that cave to this very day.

THE GALE-WUGGLE

By R. CHETWYND-HAYES

JUBILEE Tower, as one might expect, was a very tall building indeed.

Way down at ground level was a supermarket, a television hire showroom, several shops and a cinema. The next three floors housed offices of various kinds, then level upon level of flats right up to the fortieth floor. But perched on top of this human ant-hill of steel and concrete was a penthouse. Built on the roof, it was so high up, Gerald's father said he wouldn't be surprised if, come winter, they had snow on their beards.

Gerald thought this to be extremely unlikely, as neither he nor his father—and most certainly not his mother—had a beard, but he was quite prepared to see an abominable snowman wending its way between the cement tubs of flowering plants. Of course, his sister, who was all of nine years old and considered to be very advanced for her age, said this was complete nonsense, as an abominable snowman would never be allowed on the lift, and, in any case, such a creature—if it existed at all—lived far away on top of mountains that were much higher than Jubilee Tower.

Gerald could do no more than bow before such superior knowledge, but he thought that having moved up into such an elevated position, there ought to be some unusual manifestations. True that on a fine day, when his father carried him out on to that part of the roof which did duty as a garden, and he was able to peer down over the parapet, people did rather resemble ants that were looking for somewhere to hide, but he lacked the strength to stand upright for any length of time to have a really good look.

As the doctor must be a man of great learning, he decided to ask his opinion once the weekly examination was completed.

"Doctor, this is a very high building, isn't it?"

Doctor Canfield nodded his grey head.

"It certainly is, Gerald. Way up above the noise. You are very lucky."

"But shouldn't I—well—see things up here—that can't be seen down below?"

The doctor pulled the bedclothes back into position, then ruffled his hair. "Depends on what you want to see. And if you have the right kind of eyes."

"Right kind of eyes?"

"Yes. Long ago, before even I was born, my father lived in the country. He was about your age at the time. And the old folk said a colony of elves lived in a nearby wood, but the no-nonsense people just laughed and talked about superstition and fairy tales—you know the kind of thing?"

Gerald nodded. "But didn't anyone go into the woods and look for the elves?"

The doctor laughed softly. "Wouldn't have done any good if they had. They could have searched those woods from sunrise to sunset and not a solitary elf would they have seen. Hadn't got the right kind of eyes, you see."

"But your father had!" Gerald exclaimed.

"Indeed he had. Spotted their village at first glance. Told me there were three rows of little cottages, no bigger than flowerpots, nestling down between the roots of an oak tree."

Gerald pondered on this most remarkable story for some time, then he asked shyly: "Do you suppose I have the right kind of eyes?"

"I wouldn't be at all surprised. Let's have a look."

110

Doctor Canfield put on a large pair of spectacles, then peered gravely into Gerald's very wide-open eyes.

"Um. Blue—that's a hopeful sign—and round. Long lashes too. Ah! What have we here? A tiny fleck in each corner! That's it. You've definitely got seeing eyes."

Gerald said: "Gosh!" and felt very superior to his wretched sister, even if she did know where abominable snowmen lived. The doctor removed his spectacles and put them away in a leather case.

"All those eyes need is practice. Keep 'em wide open and heaven's above knows what they'll see."

Then Gerald's mother came into the bedroom, and the doctor rose rather quickly from his chair and picked up his black bag.

"Gerald and I have been chatting away and quite forgot the time, Mrs Grantworthy."

Gerald's mother creased her face into a bright smile, but he could see the anxious look in her eyes that was rarely absent these days. She said: "How nice. And he's much, much, better, isn't he, doctor?"

"Good heavens, I'll say he is! Be running up and down those confounded stairs in no time."

Then both he and Mrs Grantworthy left the room, and Gerald heard them speaking softly in the hall and once was able to understand three words: "There's always hope."

He wondered why Doctor Canfield considered it necessary to reassure his mother as to the continued existence of hope, and if it had anything to do with the anxious look in her eyes and the fact that she sometimes cried. But he had long ago given up trying to understand adults and now gave his full consideration to the subject of "seeing eyes".

The large French windows overlooked the roof, and it was obviously there that any strange manifestation would take place. From his bed he could see the cement

111

tubs in which flowering plants politely bowed their colourful heads to the prevailing breeze; and one of Marcia's dolls, that was looking rather the worse for wear after spending a rainy night on the parapet. But there was not the slightest sign of an elf.

After some thought, Gerald decided that it was unlikely that these minute people would take up residence on a cement roof. They belonged to dense woods and tall grass and would be very unhappy in these artificial surroundings. No, he must train his special eyes to see something that would be—like this abominable snowman—at home on a mountain top—or in the sky.

Gerald began to watch the sky.

"Your eyes are no different to anyone else's," Marcia protested. "And certainly not as good as mine."

"But I tell you, Doctor Canfield says I have special eyes," Gerald insisted. "Like his father, who could see elves."

Marcia smiled with gentle scorn. "That proves he was just making it up. Everybody knows that there are no such things as elves."

Gerald nodded with grave satisfaction. "That's what all no-nonsense people say. You couldn't see an elf even if you tried ever so hard."

"Oh, yes, I could."

Mrs Grantworthy, hearing the raised voices, came into the room and frowned at her young daughter.

"You're not to argue with your brother. You know he's not very strong and mustn't be excited."

"But he says he has special eyes—and he hasn't."

"Go and put your hat and coat on. Your father is waiting to drive you to school."

Marcia ran cheerfully from the room, for like all no-nonsense people, she soon forgot a disagreement and was now looking forward to the coming day. Mrs

Grantworthy smoothed Gerald's hair from his forehead and said: "You mustn't take any notice of what your sister says. She likes to tease you"

Gerald smiled complacently. "I don't. May I go out on to the roof?"

She looked enquiringly out of the window.

"It's a bit windy, dear. You mustn't catch cold."

"I won't. Not if I wear my thick dressing-gown. May I—please?"

Eventually Mrs Grantworthy gave way to his pleading—she always did—and helped him out on to the roof and into a long garden chair. There he lay back and stared up at the cloud-dappled sky. There was no manner of doubt whatsoever—he was learning to see.

Already he had come to understand that small flying objects were not always birds. If a person, gifted with the right kind of eyes, watched them through a fringe of long lashes, and concentrated really hard, then—more often that not—there was a flight of little old women gliding through the air. So far as Gerald could see, they wore tiny top hats and black cloaks that not only covered their entire bodies, but trailed out behind and on each side, so as to create the impression that these aerial creatures were equipped with triangular wings.

Sometimes they made a strange wailing sound, and Gerald would only smile when his father said: "Those crows are making an awful din," for he knew it was no use trying to explain to those who could not see. Even the doctor, on being told of the successful development of Gerald's special sight, only frowned and took his temperature.

On this particular morning, the sky resembled a bad-tempered face that might shed rain-tears at any moment, and the clouds kept surging over and under each other, so that Gerald had grave doubts if the airborne old ladies would venture out in such precarious weather. Although the wind was rising and tried to turn his hair into a gold-tinted nest, it was quite warm and did not make him cough once.

His mother called from the open window. "Don't you think you should come in, dear? I have to go out for a while and I don't want you to be caught in a rainstorm."

"No, I'll be all right," he assured her. "If it rains I can go indoors. I'm much stronger today."

"Well—if you say so. I won't be long."

Gerald lay back and watched the clouds through narrowed eyes. The wind, with the perversity of its kind, was tormenting them. They writhed, seethed, built up into great fat billows, then went tumbling across the heavens, as though trying to outrun this terrible, wailing monster.

Then Gerald saw it—*that* which can only be seen by special eyes, which is no reason to suppose it does not exist. It came sailing out of a veritable sea of boiling clouds; roughly shaped like a bull with no legs, a fleecy, white body that was dappled in places with stormy black, and with a gleaming grey streak running down the back. The face—and Gerald could clearly see every feature—was made up of jutting brows, a round snout that alternated between bright pink to vivid red, most innocent-looking blue eyes, and an extremely broad mouth. Taken by and large, he decided it really was a most beautiful creature and much more interesting than airborne little old ladies.

It glided along just under the roof of clouds, turning its head slowly from one side to another, then came to a stop above a tall building which had a flag fluttering from a green mast. There it floated, looking down with bright blue eyes upon the sprawling city. Then, suddenly, it seemed to take an exceedingly deep breath, for its mouth opened and some of the nearest clouds were

114

sucked in. The head grew larger by the second, then the body expanded until it resembled a gigantic balloon, and Gerald put shaking hands over his ears, as he fully expected to hear a mighty explosion.

Then—the air-monster blew.

A seemingly unending plume of cloud poured out of the gaping mouth, and the most terrible wind that Gerald had ever felt or heard went roaring over the rooftops, tore the flag from its mast, rushed in through one open window and played havoc with a lot of papers, then descended to street level, where it doubtlessly lifted hats and skirts without so much as a by your leave.

But Gerald—who expected to have his chair overturned at any moment—could only watch the creature who was responsible for all this commotion. As it blew, the snout grew longer, the body shrank, and the eyes took on the appearance of large blue saucers. Then, having regained its original size, it glided over the street and—to Gerald's great alarm—moved to a position immediately above Jubilee Tower.

Now he could look up at the underside of the monster, which resembled an odd-shaped cloud, and gave a loud cry of alarm when he realised that it was about to sink down and completely engulf him. The wind snatched his cry and carried it up into the tumultous heavens—and presumably into the ears of the sky-monster as well, for it bent its head and stared down at him with more than ordinary interest.

Suddenly the wind sank and became nothing more than an innocent summer breeze, which, in some strange way, slowly emerged into a sighing whisper.

"You . . . can . . . see . . . me?"

For some time Gerald was quite unable to answer this simple question, and, in fact, was not at all sure if the whispered words were not the result of his excited

The air-monster blew . . .

imagination. But when the creature continued to stare at him and appeared to be waiting for an answer, he did manage to produce a hesitant: "Y-yes."

"The breeze sighed again. "You . . . are . . . ill?"

At that moment, Mrs Grantworthy came running from the open French windows, still dressed in her outdoor clothes and clearly in a state of intense agitation. She put an arm round Gerald's shoulders and all but lifted him from the chair.

"Oh, that dreadful wind! I got back as soon as I could. Are you all right?"

"Yes, but . . ."

"Good heavens, you look so pale! Back to bed at once and I'll ring Doctor Canfield."

He was half carried, part led into his bedroom, but just managed to glance back over one shoulder and catch a glimpse of the sky-monster, which was gliding away to the west. Once in bed, Mrs Grantworthy turned on the electric blanket, then walked quickly to the telephone and dialled a number. Gerald listened to her begging Doctor Canfield to come round at once, although his thoughts were far away, following the trail of an awesome creature that rode on the back of the north wind.

His mother sank down on to a chair and watched him with anxious eyes.

"I should never have left you out there. Heavens above, you might have been blown off the roof!"

"But the sky-monster stopped the wind when it knew I was ill."

This statement, far from reassuring Mrs Grantworthy, made her clap hand to mouth and stare at him with wide-eyed horror.

"You've got a fever! Oh, why doesn't Doctor Canfield come?"

Although Gerald had never been so clear of mind, he

did feel very weak. But it was a rather pleasant sensation, as though his body had become sun-warmed mist and he might float away on a gentle breeze at any moment. Then the doorbell rang, and his mother said: "Oh, thank goodness, there he is!" before running into the hall and returning with Doctor Canfield.

The doctor put his black bag down on the table and assumed an expression of mock horror.

"What's all this then? Caught out in the freak gale, were we? My word, it was a whistler. Now, let's have a look at you."

He listened to Gerald's heartbeat through a stethoscope—which was extremely cold—then laid a cool hand on his forehead.

"No more trips out on the roof for a while, my lad."

Gerald tugged at the doctor's sleeve and waited until the tired face was bent over him. "I saw a big thing—like a bull with no legs—in the sky, and it blew so hard there was a gale."

Doctor Canfield straightened up and frowned thoughtfully.

"Did you now! That's strange."

Mrs Grantworthy shook her head in mock reproof. "Your imagination, Gerald! You mustn't take any notice, Doctor."

The doctor waved his hand impatiently. "No, wait a minute. My father told me an old folk tale which was about a strange sky-monster that looked like a bull with no legs. I gather he got it from the old woman who looked after him and his twin brother. It was called—it's on the tip of my tongue—the . . . the Gale-Wuggle. That's it-the Gale-Wuggle. Ever heard that name before, Gerald?"

Gerald shook his head. "No. Never. But I really did see it. And it spoke to me. A kind of whisper. Sort of sigh-talking."

118

"Has he got a fever?" Mrs Grantworthy asked.

"Maybe a slight one—which might account for monsters in the sky. But—a Gale-Wuggle! Well—keep him warm, Mrs Grantworthy. I'll pop in again tomorrow."

When his mother conducted Doctor Canfield to the door, Gerald closed his eyes and tried to imagine where the Gale-Wuggle was now. It must be tired after all that blowing and would probably have to curl up on a fleecy cloud and sleep for several days.

Presently, Gerald too fell asleep and dreamed he was riding on the Gale-Wuggle's back, through a blue meadow, which shimmered under a rainbow-coloured sky.

Three days later the weather became hot and sunny, and the doctor said Gerald could get out of bed, so long as he did not walk about too much. So he sat in his garden chair and looked up with almost breathless expectancy, but, of course, there was no wind worth mentioning, or even the smallest cloud, and the prospect of the Gale-Wuggle turning up in a clear sky was very remote. But the airborne old ladies were out in force; entire droves flew in arrow-head formations and appeared to be in a hurry to get somewhere. Others were diving, flying round in circles, and Gerald could not dismiss the thought that they were—well—sort of young old ladies. Some chased each other and made shrill wailing sounds that were not dissimilar to a whistling kettle demanding attention.

Then one dived down to roof-level and came gliding in Gerald's direction, making him gasp when it settled on the parapet and stared at him with tiny, red eyes. He had never seen such an ugly creature before. At close view it became apparent that the top hat and cloak were part of the minute monster—an extension of its body— and could never be removed. The face was dead white,

119

surrounded by a mane of matted grey hair, and the nose resembled a hooked, yellow beak that almost touched the jutting chin. Then a tiny claw came out and pointed a shaking forefinger at Gerald, while the creature emitted a sound that was not far removed from a cackling laugh.

Despite the blazing sun and the stifling heat, Gerald shivered and would have got up and run into the penthouse, had he found the strength to do so. But he could only sit in his chair and hope the nasty little thing would fly away. But it suddenly raised its voice to a shrill shriek, and several more of the airborne little old ladies swooped down and settled on the parapet. They all sat in a long line and watched him with red, unblinking eyes, the black cloaks clinging to their bent little bodies like folded wings.

Such a spectacle was too much for Gerald, particularly as there was no indication as to what these creatures intended to do next, so he called out: "Help me! Help me!"—not that he really expected anyone to come to his assistance, as Mrs Grantworthy was out shopping. Then suddenly—literally out of a clear sky—came a mighty clap of thunder, followed by a bellowing roar that might have been caused by a passing gale. Instantly there was a united chorus of squawks, agitated flapping of wings, and the entire hideous pack rose up from the parapet and soon became black specks that disappeared behind the distant power station.

After due consideration and careful examination of the now empty sky, Gerald called out: "Thank you, Gale-Wuggle," and felt very happy when a gentle breeze caressed his hair.

Doctor Canfield nodded thoughtfully. "Little airborne old ladies, you say! 'Pon my soul! And dressed in cloaks and top hats! Goodness gracious! They could be banshees."

120

"But the Gale-Wuggle drove them away," Gerald pointed out. "Does that mean it likes me?"

The doctor slipped his stethoscope into a side pocket and shrugged. "It would appear so. Mind you, I've always understood that a Gale-Wuggle made people disappear. Sort of came down on top of 'em. But I suppose it has likes and dislikes and could well have taken a fancy to you."

Mrs Grantworthy was clearly not at all happy with this conversation and hastened to register an objection.

"Don't you think that Gerald should be discouraged in these fanciful notions, Doctor? I'm sure they can't be good for him."

"Imagination is a good friend, so long as it provides a happy ending," the doctor retorted. "And Gerald's Gale-Wuggle certainly did that. But it is extraordinary how he manages to describe these creatures, when, so far as I can understand, he has never read or heard about them. I mean to say, there isn't one person in a hundred thousand who even knows about a Gale-Wuggle."

"I still think he should read a nice book," Mrs Grantworthy insisted. "It really is most disturbing to hear him talking about horrible things that float in the sky, and awful little old ladies who wear top hats."

But Gerald could not wait for the next windy day, even though his special eyes had by now become so keen he was able to see much that had been hidden from him up to now. There were, for example, the tiny people who came out from the wainscotting and played hide-and-seek in the hearthrug. And the long, almost transparent, snakelike thing, that undulated through the air and sometimes draped itself round the ceiling lamp. But he was fast getting used to this kind of thing and nothing— not even the disembodied head that rose up from the floor and disappeared through the ceiling—could rival the great Gale-Wuggle that rode in on the north wind.

So the long, hot, summer days slid out, one after the other, from the great storehouse of time, and Gerald grew a little stronger and was able to stand up and look down over the parapet. Toy cars continued to race along a narrow grey ribbon of road, and ant-like people scurried here and there, not one of whom knew or cared about the existence of a Gale-Wuggle. And the dazzling blue sky was like a vast steel dome that permitted only the stray passing bird, or a roaring jet plane to disturb its serenity.

Then one day Mr Grantworthy—after a long talk with Doctor Canfield—came into Gerald's bedroom and said: "Seaside for you, my lad. Sea air will set you up in no time."

Normally Gerald would have been very excited at this prospect, but now he felt a strange reluctance to leave his rooftop home and forego the weekly visits of Doctor Canfield, who was the only person he could confide in. Also, would the Gale-Wuggle know where he had gone? But there was no argument that would prevail against his parents—and Marcia's—enthusiasm. Mrs Grantworthy spoke of cool sea breezes, Mr Grantworthy of wonderful castles that could be built of sand, and Marcia went into a state of disgusting rapture when she pondered on the delights of wearing a straw hat and bathing her feet in salt water.

Cases were packed, milk and newspapers cancelled for two weeks, electricity switched off at the main, then Gerald was helped into the lift by his father and finally made comfortable on the back seat of the family car. Marcia sat in the far corner and loudly proclaimed her impatience when they were held up in a traffic jam, their father shouted at several motorists who refused to allow him to overtake, and Mrs Grantworthy expressed grave concern that so many drivers had not bothered to learn the highway code. All in all, it was a fairly normal journey.

When they arrived at Mrs Brown's Guest House, that good lady welcomed them on the doorway and said how nice it was to see them again and how well Gerald was looking—under the circumstances. He was installed in a front bedroom, which commanded a fine view of the sea, and at once developed a keen interest in the scene laid out before him. The beach was packed with holiday-makers. Elderly gentlemen sat in deck chairs with white handkerchiefs draped over their peeling faces; young ladies in bikinis lay roasting on the golden sand; and children screamed with delight when small, well-behaved waves chased them back to the shore. But it was the *other* beings that attracted Gerald's special sight.

Little grey and white creatures, that might have been mistaken for seagulls were it not for their tiny old-man heads, flew round and round and gave out mournful cries, that Gerald gradually translated into two drawn-out words.

"We're . . . lost . . ."

He wished Doctor Canfield had been present, for that clever person would doubtlessly have known what these creatures were. But his mother may have unwittingly revealed the truth when, at dinner that night, she said plaintively: "What an awful noise those seagulls make. Really, they sound like lost souls."

Gerald wondered how souls became lost and if they would ever find themselves again. But next day, when he was taken down to the beach and seated in a deck chair, it became apparent that they were not the only unusual phenomenon that existed in the land of sea and sunshine.

Sometimes a faint mist would rise up from the ocean and become a bright oval shape that took on all the colours of the rainbow. Then the lost souls—if that was what they were—tried to fly into the oval; became a

123

mass of flapping wings and screaming faces, looking rather like a rush-hour crowd, all attempting to board a train at once.

And those that got in, never came out. After a short while, the oval shape dissolved back into mist, which sank into the sea, and the lost souls which had not made a successful entry, wailed their grief and flew round in ever-increasing circles, as though hoping it would reappear from a different place. But Gerald never saw it more than once a day.

Then clouds rolled a thick, grey blanket over the sun, and a cold wind transformed the gentle waves into roaring, foam-tipped monsters, that pounded the beach and tried to leap up on to the pier. Rain drove the erstwhile sunbathers into boarding house or hotel, and Mrs Brown was heard to remark: "When it rains by the sea—it rains."

Gerald's newly acquired strength waned with the dying summer, and he lay in bed and listened to the wailing wind, which sometimes was blended with the despairing cry of lost souls. That was not the only sound he heard. During the long night hours, when either his father or mother kept watch beside his bed, he would shiver when a banshee howled from just beyond his curtained window and murmur: "Why doesn't the Gale-Wuggle come?"

His father, not believing, but wishing to comfort, said gently: "It will come, son. Have no fear it will come."

But would it find him here, in this house which was only two storeys high? Should one not be up on the roof of the world when the Gale-Wuggle sailed the stormy skies? Then he remembered that day when the banshees had perched on the parapet and they had been frightened away by the clap of thunder and the sudden roar of the wind. He had sent out an appeal for help, and the Gale-Wuggle must have heard, even though

124

there wasn't a cloud in the sky. Suppose he tried again? Only not aloud, lest his mother become even more anxious, and his father send for the strange doctor, who was undoubtedly a no-nonsense person.

So Gerald sent out a silent message. He *thought*: "Gale-Wuggle, I am very ill. Please come . . . please come," and slipped into a dreamless sleep immediately afterwards.

He was awakened by the howling wind and lay quite still, trying to remember where he was. Then it all came back. He was in Mrs Brown's Guest House and he was ill, which was not unusual, only now he was much worse than ever before. He turned his head. Mrs Grantworthy was asleep in her chair. Head lowered, eyes closed, she was breathing heavily, worn out by three nights of continuous watching. Gerald supposed his father must be resting in the next room.

Then he heard the wind sink down to a loud whisper. "Come . . . out . . . out . . ."

But how could he go out, when he scarcely had the strength to raise his head? He whispered: "I can't. Honestly, I can't."

The wind rose a little, and the whisper was transformed into an impatient growl.

"You . . . can . . . can . . ."

Gerald eased back the bedclothes and swung one leg down to the floor. Then he rested, taking deep breaths and watching his mother with great anxiety, for it was so important that she did not wake up. When he stood up, the room seemed to wobble from side to side, and the floor heaved in a most alarming fashion. Taking the first step was a perilous adventure, and the next a well-planned excercise. Then he reached the door where there was some difficulty, for he was obliged to cling to the doorpost with one hand, while turning the handle with the other.

Fortunately Mrs Brown left a light burning on the landing and in the hall, so Gerald could see quite clearly, as he clung to the banisters and went downstairs, one step at a time. Once down in the hall, he had to rest again and try to control his gasping breath and thumping heart, before tackling the double-bolted front door.

Easing each bolt from its socket was an awful job. They groaned so loudly, Gerald fully expected Mrs Brown to appear at any moment and demand to know what he was doing; and it was fully five minutes before he could turn the big brass handle and pull the door inwards. Then he staggered out into the wind-haunted night and held on to one of the pillars which supported the porch.

After a while he looked up.

The Gale-Wuggle was a scant three metres above the ground; the great bull-shaped mass a silhouette against the cloud-embattled moon, the head bent forward and the blue, luminous eyes looking downwards. Gerald knew they were watching him. The wind became a moaning sigh.

"Come . . . e . . . e . . . e . . . e . . ."

The Gale-Wuggle turned and glided towards the sea, and Gerald realised he must follow, even if it meant crawling across the road and on to the beach. But as he stepped down on to the pavement, it seemed as if the wind had formed a pair of strong arms that held him upright and, at the same time, propelled him forward. As Gerald lurched across the road, he heard a beautiful voice, that was sometimes just over his head, but at others was far away, singing the following words:

"It roams over land, air and sea.
'Tis whatever you wish it to be.
To the evil it's bad:

126

> To the mournful it's sad
> But those in distress
> Will find immediate redress,
> When they call upon the Gale-Wuggle."

Then he was lying on soft sand, and the night was suddenly without sound, save for the gentle murmur of tumbling waves that were rocking the sea to sleep. The moon came out from behind a cloud and turned the Gale-Wuggle into a glorious, silver-trimmmed creature that had been created from the fabric of dreams, but would always be seen by those who have not been tainted by no-nonsense, I-don't-believe-it, it-stands-to-reason and other despicable terms. The large face looked down on Gerald and never before had he seen such an expression of compassion and love.

Slowly the gleaming body came lower—and lower—and Gerald was not in the least afraid, knowing that far from harming him, the Gale-Wuggle had the kindest intentions. Gradually he was enveloped in a warm mist, that seemed to seep into his lungs, pour along his bloodstream, do something wonderful to his liver and kidneys, and finally send him into a deep, health-giving sleep.

"An absolute miracle," Mr Grantworthy exclaimed for the seventh time. "There's no other word for it."

"And I thought he was dead," Mrs Grantworthy said, wiping her eyes on a lace handkerchief. "Lying out there so still. And when I found his bed empty . . ."

"Never mind," Mr Grantworthy consoled her. "All's well that ends well."

"Of course," the strange doctor looked superciliously down his nose, "these so-called miraculous cures always have a scientific explanation if one cares to investigate."

127

Gerald had just finished eating an enormous breakfast and was looking forward to an entire day on the beach, where he would outrun, outswim and out-everything-else that little wretch Marcia. But it was necessary to at least try and convince these well-meaning, but so stupid adults of what really happened.

"It was the Gale-Wuggle. I called it last night and it made me go outside, then it came down on top of me and . . ."

"What a wonderful imagination," Mr Grantworthy rudely interrupted. "Takes after me, I shouldn't wonder."

The strange, no-nonsense doctor nodded. "Utter rot, of course, but quite amusing. Shouldn't be surprised if he becomes one of those writer chaps when he grows up."

"But it's all true," Gerald insisted. "Please believe me."

"Oh, look, there's a bright colour in his cheeks," Mrs Grantworthy cried. "Oh dear, I do believe I'm going to faint."

She did—for the third time that morning. Gerald gave up. What was the use? None were so blind as those who had no eyes. He could have told the doctor about the tiny banshee that sat on his left shoulder, but this enlightening—if not encouraging—information would not have been received with the gravity it deserved. It would also be a waste of time to mention that a veritable army of tiny, transparent things was swarming over the bedside cabinet and trying to pull the lamp over.

"When I grow up," he told himself, "I will become a "writer chap" and tell everyone about the Gale-Wuggle."

And he did.